"Do you have any weapons?"

Huang pulled back his jacket, exposing a Walther PPK .380.

"I've got one, too." Kelly began to dig through her handbag.

Bolan glanced at his watch. It was 16:25. They had a few more hours until Grimaldi's flight was scheduled to land. "Let's go check out the prison. I want to see what we're dealing with."

Huang and Kelly exchanged a look. Bolan sensed they were holding something back. He stared at Huang. "What else do you want to tell me?"

Huang glanced at the woman again, licked his lips, then said, "When Wayne and I were talking to Han, he refused to go with us. He insisted he has to stay in China until he gets some issues resolved. He just wants to make sure his family is safe."

"He's not worried about his impending arrest?"

Huang shrugged. "He said he had some kind of... insurance policy."

Recycling programs
for this product may
not exist in your area.

First edition February 2015

ISBN-13: 978-0-373-64435-3

Special thanks and acknowledgment to
Michael A. Black for his contribution to this work.

Dragon Key

0 1021 0288058 4

Printed in U.S.A.

Three may keep a secret, if two of them are dead.
—Benjamin Franklin,
Poor Richard's Almanack

Nothing is more dangerous than someone whose ugly
secrets are about to be revealed. But once the truth
comes out, it's time for justice.
—Mack Bolan

THE
MACK BOLAN
LEGEND

Nothing less than a war could have fashioned the destiny of the man called Mack Bolan. Bolan earned the Executioner title in the jungle hell of Vietnam.

But this soldier also wore another name—Sergeant Mercy. He was so tagged because of the compassion he showed to wounded comrades-in-arms and Vietnamese civilians.

Mack Bolan's second tour of duty ended prematurely when he was given emergency leave to return home and bury his family, victims of the Mob. Then he declared a one-man war against the Mafia.

He confronted the Families head-on from coast to coast, and soon a hope of victory began to appear. But Bolan had broken society's every rule. That same society started gunning for this elusive warrior—to no avail.

So Bolan was offered amnesty to work within the system against terrorism. This time, as an employee of Uncle Sam, Bolan became Colonel John Phoenix. With a command center at Stony Man Farm in Virginia, he and his new allies—Able Team and Phoenix Force—waged relentless war on a new adversary: the KGB.

But when his one true love, April Rose, died at the hands of the Soviet terror machine, Bolan severed all ties with Establishment authority.

Now, after a lengthy lone-wolf struggle and much soul-searching, the Executioner has agreed to enter an "arm's-length" alliance with his government once more, reserving the right to pursue personal missions in his Everlasting War.

Prologue

Hong Kong, warehouse district

It was a matter of honor, the Praying Mantis thought as he moved in the semidarkness of the alley. That was how Mr. Chen, his master, had described this mission to him. Honor and tradition... Two things that were very important to the Triad, and thus to the Mantis, as well.

Duty is preceded by honor, he thought.

He dragged his left foot and leaned heavily on a long walking stick. Just another Hong Kong beggar out for a night's work, going through garbage cans and asking for handouts. The long overcoat felt cumbersome, but it was a necessary disguise. He mimicked a limp as he drew nearer to the rear entrance of the warehouse, closer to the two guards who stood there in their casual contempt. They were young Chinese, cocky and full of themselves. Chong should have chosen better. They both wore finely tailored navy suits with black silk ties and sunglasses, even though it was close to midnight and the sun would not shine again for hours. For these two it was all about the image. Chinese gangsters trying to emulate what they saw in some John Woo movie. All image and no substance. The Mantis flexed his abdominal muscles in anticipation, but he doubted these two would present much of a problem. Vanity was not a desirable quality in an enforcer or bodyguard. Sunglasses at night.

It doesn't matter, the Mantis thought. The sun will never shine upon them again.

He stepped closer, leaning on the long stick, still dragging his left foot, his face streaked like a tiger with black camo paint.

"Can you spare some change for a poor, old, crippled man?" he said in a distorted voice, imbuing the Mandarin with a rural twang. He let his lips creep into a smile as he moved within striking distance, holding out his cupped palm.

The closest one twisted his mouth into a snarl as he stepped out from the doorway and cocked back his hand, ready to deliver a harsh blow to the old beggar.

"Get out of here, you peasant son-of-a—"

The Mantis thrust the fingers of his cupped hand upward into the soft area at the base of the guard's neck. As the man made a gurgling sound and stumbled to the side, the Mantis pivoted to the left, bringing the stick upward with three consecutive blows, striking the second guard's groin, abdomen and throat. The Mantis pivoted again, this time to the right, using a spinning back kick. The heel of his right foot smashed into the first guard's face and the man crumpled. The second guard was on his knees, struggling to reach under the lapel of his finely tailored suit when the Mantis delivered a lightning-quick blow—a palm strike to the side of the man's head—sending his temple crashing into the sharp edges of the brick doorway. He collapsed to the ground, as well.

After assuring himself that both men were dead, the Mantis dragged the bodies behind a pair of garbage cans and quickly went through their pockets. He removed a pistol from each and a radio from the second man. The Mantis dropped the weapons into the pockets of his overcoat and held the radio in his hand as he went back to the door. It was unlocked.

He slipped into the dark interior and divested himself of the heavy overcoat and stick. It would be close quarters from this point onward. Underneath the overcoat he wore his customary working clothes: a black jumpsuit made of soft, double-knit fabric that allowed for his high kicks and quick movements. Over the jumpsuit was a leather vest equipped with several slit-like pockets, each pocket containing a special weapon. The Mantis had heard that in olden times, a Triad enforcer's vest would be lined with finely wrought iron mesh. Despite his affinity for tradition, this vest was lined with Kevlar. As he stood in the darkness, letting his eyes adjust, he thought about taking the guns but decided to leave them. This was, after all, a matter of honor. The traditional ways should dominate.

The Mantis stepped forward, the soles of his shoes making virtually no sound as he moved over the solid concrete floor. The warehouse was fully stocked with barrels of rice, but devoid of workers. He imagined Chong had paid off any security guards so the meeting could continue unobstructed. Chong was thorough, but like most traitors, not thorough enough. Following the five of them from the docks had been almost too easy.

He heard their voices now.... Low, guttural sounds interspersed with laughter. Several men were talking, more concerned with money than vigilance. The Mantis moved soundlessly down an aisle with metal barrels stacked on either side.

The voices grew louder. More laughing. One of them

was Chong. The Mantis was sure of it. At the corner he paused and flattened against the barrels, tilting his head slightly so he could glance down the aisle. A man stood at the other end, perhaps ten meters away, his silhouette in a position of alertness, holding a submachine gun.

The Mantis smiled. This guard, too, was wearing sunglasses.

Moving behind the wall of barrels, the Mantis flicked the outside pocket of the vest and felt the sharpened edge of a throwing dart. This guard was a large man, probably chosen for intimidation rather than his skill, but size did not always matter. The Mantis cocked his arm and closed his eyes for a moment of concentration.

He opened his eyes, stepped to his left using a smooth, fluid movement and threw the dart. A split second later the guard's head jerked back, the jagged edge of the throwing dart protruding from the opaque lens over his left eye. His hand started up toward his head but stopped. His mouth sagged open, dribbling a trail of blood. As the big guard began to fall forward, the Mantis covered the distance between them and caught the man before he hit the floor. With a quick finger jab to the man's throat, the Mantis made sure the guard would not recover. The guard made a short choking sound, a death rattle, and was silent. The Mantis laid him onto the cold concrete floor and removed the machine gun from the dead man's hands. It was an HK MP5. A fine weapon, but he set it aside.

"Make them suffer for their treachery," Master Chen had said. "Make an example of them."

The Mantis peered around the edge of the stacked barrels. One more guard stood perhaps fifteen meters away, holding another MP5. A portable light had been set up in the middle of a clear section of the floor. Chong and another man sat in the bright circle of light at a small folding table piled with stacks of money. This second man wore tiny oval glasses as his fingers worked nimbly over an abacus. Leo Kim, Mr. Chen's personal accountant in Hong Kong. This was an unexpected development. Two traitors would die tonight.

The Mantis removed another dart then scanned the surroundings. Nothing moved in the shadows of the warehouse. The two men's voices, their laughter, their squeals of delight as they counted the money, floated from the table like joyful butterflies.

This guard should be the last one, the Mantis thought. Kim would be too scared to bring any associates. He was a mouse, feeding on the crumbs left by others.

The Mantis traced his thumb over the sharpened point of the dart, the finely honed edge grating softly against each minute ridgeline. He breathed in and out, listening, melting into the darkness and shadows, watching, waiting...

Something flickered on the other side of the room. A man, another guard, stood in the shadows. He stepped forward and the Mantis appraised him: well muscled, dark clothing and no sunglasses decorating his pockmarked face. This one was obviously in charge. The boss guard. He raised a portable radio to his mouth and asked, "Deng, do you see anything?"

The Mantis stepped back. Perhaps it would be prudent to use one of the guns after all. This new guard was obviously more competent than the others. Kim must have brought him along, just in case. The mouse bringing a cat to keep him safe. The irony was obvious. This bastard would probably just as soon cut Kim's throat and steal his money as protect him.

The room grew silent. No one had responded. The

boss guard spoke into the radio again. "Deng, you idiot, where the hell are you?"

The seconds ticked by with no answer.

The Mantis thought again about picking up the sub-machine gun. But his master's honor was at stake. Mr. Chen was not his *sifu,* but Chen had taken him in from the streets, raised him, taught him the way of the Triad and the code of the warrior and had made sure he had the best schooling in all manners of martial combat.

The Mantis took out another dart.

The boss guard reached inside his jacket and pulled out a stainless steel, semiauto Norinco Type 54 pistol as he stepped into the circle of light and toward the other guard, who was now gripping his submachine gun with both hands.

The Norinco's shiny finish gleamed in the harsh light. The Mantis liked shiny things.

"See if everything's all right," the boss guard said. "Find out why they aren't answering. And take off those damn sunglasses."

The other guard nodded and turned, his dominant hand pulling the glasses off. As he did so, the Mantis stepped forward and threw the first dart. The guard's hand froze in front of his face, still holding the glasses, the end of the dart protruding from his right eye socket. He sunk to his knees and fell forward, his face smacking against the concrete.

The boss guard raised his pistol, but it was too late. The second dart was already on its way, striking him in the neck, just below his jawbone. He twisted and reached for the dart, firing off a few quick but random shots.

The Mantis burst forward, taking three long, running steps and jumping in the air. He sailed past Kim and clipped Chong with a flying kick. Landing on the other side of the table, the Mantis delivered a three-kick combination to the gurgling boss guard. The last round-house kick smacked against the man's throat, driving the dart in deeper and sending him toppling backward. The Mantis glanced at the two traitors. Chong was shaking his head, trying to clear it. Kim, the mouse, just sat there holding his hands in front of his face, which held an image of frozen horror. Shifting on the balls of his feet, the Mantis delivered three successive back-fist blows to Chong's face, and then he swept a knife-hand back and smashed Kim's nose, sending his glasses askew and knocking him to the ground.

The Mantis flicked his hand to another pocket of the vest and withdrew a folding knife. A butterfly, or *balisong,* as the Filipinos called it. It was not a Chinese weapon, but it was one of the Mantis's favorites. He'd grown up watching Hong Kong actors manipulate the handles and blades in martial arts movies, and had adopted the knife as his own.

Flipping the *balisong* open with one hand, he whirled and stepped over the boss guard's supine body. The man appeared to be dead, but the Mantis slashed his throat just to be sure.

Chong was on all fours, groaning and trying to get to his feet. The Mantis stepped back and sent a quick, thrusting front kick to the side of Chong's head. He collapsed. The traitor appeared to be unconscious as the Mantis checked him for weapons and found a small, silver-colored .380 in his jacket pocket. The Mantis recognized the gun. Chen had given it to Chong when he'd first joined the Triad.

I will return it to the master, the Mantis thought.

Dropping Chong's limp form, the Mantis reached

down and grabbed the front of Kim's shirt, pulling the accountant toward him.

"You had Mr. Chen's trust," the Mantis said, twisting the shirt so it choked off Kim's air supply. "He will not be pleased when he hears of your betrayal."

"I did not know," Kim said, his voice creaking between gasps.

The Mantis cast a quick glance at the stacks of money, the open briefcases and the abacus. "You didn't know…"

Kim nodded rapidly, his head bobbling up and down like a toy doll on a spring.

"So you brought your abacus to count roaches in this warehouse?" the Mantis said. He pulled the accountant closer. "You have betrayed my master, and you've offended me with your puerile lies." He put the point of his knife to the accountant's neck. "You deserve to die slowly for your treachery, but luck has favored you tonight, old man."

Kim blinked and his lips twisted into something resembling a hopeful smile.

"You'll spare me?" he asked. His eyes glowed with a sudden hopefulness.

The Mantis stared back. "No, you will die quickly instead of slowly." He plunged the blade into the softness of Kim's neck, watching the expression of hope fall away, accompanied by the fading light in the other man's eyes.

The Mantis dropped the accountant and turned to Chong, who had regained consciousness but was still on the floor. He looked upward with an expression of terror, then his mouth twitched slightly.

"Lee Son Shin?" Chong said. "Is that you?"

The Mantis said nothing.

"Lee, it's me. Chong Se Hu." He flashed a nervous smile.

The Mantis remained silent.

"Help me," Chong said. "Please. Let me go."

The Mantis did not move.

"Please, Lee." Chong managed to sit up, get to his hands and knees. "We're friends. Like brothers."

"Brothers do not disgrace themselves for a bowl of rice," the Mantis said. "Stay on your knees."

Chong's face twisted into a grimace. His eyes stared up at the Mantis, then his lips parted in a sly smile. "You're angry, aren't you? I don't blame you. But look." He managed to steady himself and gestured toward the stacks of money. "There's enough there for both of us. Enough to start over, in another place. We can both be rich men. No more taking orders, risking our lives. A chance to start over. For Son Yin, as well."

The Mantis glared down at him. "Do not mention her name."

Chong looked up, his eyes widening. "Don't you see?"

"I see a traitor," the Mantis said. "One who must be punished."

"Lee, no. Please. No." Chong bowed his head. "I beg you."

Tears rolled down the other man's cheeks.

"How much did they pay you?" the Mantis asked. "The Iranians."

Chong shook his head. "More than you can imagine. Take the money, Lee. Take it all, but please, let me live. We're friends."

The Mantis watched Chong grovel, remembering their shared childhood in Beijing. The long journey together… After his parents died, the Mantis, his sister and Chong had sneaked onto train after train until they'd arrived in Hong Kong. They'd lived on the streets before Master Chen had found them. Chong had been the first one Chen had discovered and assisted, then Chong had opened the door for Lee. But now none of that was important. All that mattered was duty and honor.

"Do not disgrace yourself further," the Mantis said. "Show me your fidelity."

Chong, the tears still streaming down his face, raised his left hand, curving his little finger under and extending the other three in a gesture indicating loyalty. The Mantis watched the traitor, letting the gravity of his betrayal, and the knowledge of what was to come, settle over him like a shroud.

"Please, Lee," Chong said. "At least make it quick."

The Mantis watched the blade gleaming in the artificial light a few seconds more, and then grabbed the three extended fingers with his left hand.

"I will," he said, and squeezed the handles of the *balisong* tightly.

1

Victoria Harbour, Hong Kong, commercial waterfront district

Mack Bolan, aka the Executioner, watched as four men removed a large wooden crate from a black truck. A fifth man stood guard, holding a pistol with a sound suppressor by his side. Bolan was standing in the shadows perhaps forty feet away, flattened against the edge of an abutment. He could hear the men speaking Farsi. So far Brognola's intel had panned out: these Iranians were up to something in Hong Kong. The five of them had met with a group of Chinese men, Triads from the looks of them, and exchanged a suitcase for the small black truck. Then both groups had gone their separate ways. It had been a juggling act for Bolan to keep both groups under surveillance, even with an assist from MI6. At this point, the lead British agent, John Crissey, had no choice but to split up his team, sending two of his men to follow the Triads with the suitcase while he and Bolan continued with the Iranians.

Crissey kept in radio contact with his men as he and Bolan trailed the truck through the busy night traffic. When the Iranians suddenly pulled into a back alley, Bolan got out of the car and tailed them on foot. They pulled up beside a parked van facing the opposite direction and Bolan gave Crissey a heads-up.

"Get on the other side of this alley," Bolan said into his throat mic. "They've got another vehicle, a blue van, ready to head out."

"Righto, Cooper," the Englishman said. As usual, Bolan was using his Matt Cooper alias. Once again he pondered the wisdom of working with MI6, but this time he'd had little choice. They were the established agency in what was once the British territory of Hong Kong, and according to Hal Brognola, Bolan was the only effective asset in the area. If he was in the neighborhood, a nearby assignment was usually waiting in the wings. But all things considered, Crissey and his guys were turning out to be competent and trustworthy.

The Iranians carried the long crate to the rear of the van. It took all of their focus, and Bolan used the opportunity to sneak closer. The Iranians slid the wooden crate inside and three of them hopped in the back with it. The other two slammed the van's rear doors. They spoke again and looked back at the small truck they'd gotten from the Triads before going around to the front of the van and getting in. It appeared they were going to abandon the black truck. A good move, just in case the Triad had rigged it with an IED or GPS. The van's engine rolled over and caught. They were taking off. It would be nicer to follow them to their ultimate destination, but Bolan figured it was time to move, in case they lost the van in the Hong Kong traffic. Bolan keyed his radio and spoke into his throat mic.

"Crissey, target's getting ready to move. You in position?"

"Affirmative."

"Let's hit them now."

"Agreed. Heading in from the far end."

That was all Bolan needed to hear. It was risky for the two of them to tackle five men who were no doubt armed, but it was also necessary if the intel Stony Man Farm had received was correct: the Iranians were purportedly buying the guidance system for one of China's DF-21D anti-ship ballistic missiles. The kind the US designated as a "carrier killer."

Hal Brognola had been most persuasive. "I don't need to tell you how worried the Navy is about this one. It's bad enough that the Chinese have them, but if they're selling the technology to the Iranians, our ships will be sitting ducks in the Persian Gulf."

Bolan knew Brognola was right. They couldn't afford to let that kind of technology fall into the Ayatollah's hands. Still, from what Bolan knew of the Chinese, the possibility that they'd export their technology to the Muslims seemed dubious.

"Cooper," Crissey said over the radio. "I'm pulling my vehicle up to block the mouth of the alley. Are you ready?"

"Roger that," Bolan said, and sprang from the shadows. "Moving in now."

He was wearing black cargo pants and a BDU shirt that fit loosely enough to hide the shoulder rig with his Beretta 93R. He'd forgone combat boots for a lighter sport tactical boot, which afforded him traction and mobility as well as soundless movement. They also packed a pretty good wallop. Bolan pulled the Beretta out of its holster and increased his pace, centering himself directly behind the windowless van so he'd be less visible in the side mirrors. The van began to accelerate toward the mouth of the alley. Bolan ran faster, nearing an all-out sprint. If Crissey wasn't in position, or if the

Iranians decided to ram the Englishman's car, things could get dicey.

Then the red flashes of brake lights glowed ahead and the van began to slow down. Bolan flipped the selector to auto as he got within two feet of the back of the van. Reaching out, he grabbed the door handle and yanked it open, raising the Beretta at the same time. The door popped open, but the van jerked to a stop, sending the Executioner slamming against the rear door. The impact felt like a body blow from a wrecking ball. Bolan fell to the ground, rolling to minimize the impact. Just as he came to a stop, he glanced toward the van. Bolan could see the illumination from a pair of headlights. Crissey had pulled his damn car front first into the alley. Tactically, it wasn't a bad move, if you were in the car. The engine block would provide the maximum ballistic cover from any gunfire emanating from the van, and it would certainly be more difficult for the van to knock the car out of the way, but the flip side was that Bolan's position was now lit up like a Hong Kong business district. And there was nowhere to go on either side.

The right rear door opened a crack and the barrel of an SKS rifle emerged. The muzzle flash burst like an exploding star as Bolan rolled away from the rounds bouncing off the pavement. He aimed the Beretta at the solid top of the door, approximating where he thought the assailant's upper body might be, and fired off three quick bursts. Luckily he'd loaded this magazine with armor-piercing bullets.

Neat round holes perforated the door in a semicircular pattern. Seconds later the rifle dropped to the ground, followed by a slumping body.

One down and three to go, Bolan thought. He wanted at least one of the Iranians alive.

As the van began backing up, the left rear door opened and the barrel of another SKS poked out.

Alive—only if possible, Bolan thought, and began rolling again.

The van's front wheels twisted, and it veered toward him, its side striking the wall of the building next to Bolan. The rifle began spitting a deadly stream of bullets, but the rounds went wide as the vehicle abraded the brick wall.

No place to hide now. Bolan sprang to his feet, firing off another burst from his Beretta. He began running. If he could get back to the small truck the Iranians had abandoned he might be able to avoid getting run over or crushed.

Or shot, he thought as another staccato burst sounded behind him. He extended his arm back to fire another burst, buying a few seconds respite.

But the van was right behind him, maybe ten feet away now, sending out a shower of sparks as it scraped against the stone wall.

Five feet.

Three.

Just as he thought it was over, the top of the van collided with a protruding section of bricks, sending out a shower of debris like pellets in a hailstorm. The van careened left, then cut right again, giving Bolan a chance to slip into a shadowy recess along the wall. He flattened against the cold bricks and the van barreled past him, its right-side mirror snapping off as it caught the edge of the alcove. Bolan waited a second more, then brought the Beretta up and fired as the front of the vehicle came into view. A series of bullet holes dappled the windshield and the driver jerked backward. The van slowed. Bolan acquired a sight picture on the front passenger and fired another three-round burst. That man slumped forward and the van decelerated, slowing to a stop.

Bolan rushed to the front of the vehicle and suddenly felt a round zoom by him. He saw movement inside the van but no muzzle flash. It had come from behind him.

Crissey.

Bolan glanced back and saw the Englishman holding a Walther PPS in his left hand and practically covering his face with his right.

"Hold your fire," Bolan yelled, hoping Crissey could hear him.

The Executioner saw two men moving inside the back of the van. One had a rifle and the other a pistol. Bolan fired another three-round burst through the pockmarked windshield and darted to the side. He reached into the pocket of his BDU shirt and pulled out a stun grenade. Hooking the round pin on the edge of the protruding bumper, Bolan pulled the pin out and rose up, smashing the driver's-side window with his Beretta.

A round zoomed past him, this time from inside the van.

"Crissey," Bolan yelled, "now would be a good time to shoot."

The Englishman rose up and fired off a volley of several rounds. Bolan tossed the grenade through the broken window and ducked down. Four seconds later the inside of the van exploded with smoke and light, accompanied by a concussive blast. Bolan moved to the rear of the vehicle and tore open the back door. The interior was filled with a cloud of smoke and the acrid smell of burned gunpowder. The last two Iranians squirmed on the floor next to the crate. Bolan grabbed the first one by the ankle and pulled him out of the van. He dropped to the ground.

Crissey was next to Bolan now, and the Executioner told him to check and secure the prisoner. Then Bolan reached for the second man's twitching feet, but the Iranian responded with a kick. The man sat up holding a pistol with an elongated barrel, pointing it directly at Crissey. Bolan fired a round into the Iranian's forehead, and he slumped to the floor. The Executioner stitched the man with another quick burst and pulled his body from the back of the vehicle.

"Thanks," Crissey said. He flashed an expression somewhere between a grimace and a grin. "And I'm sorry about that near miss when you popped up before."

"Forget it," Bolan said, moving his head slightly, trying to clear the ringing in his ears. "You got that guy cuffed?"

"Righto."

Bolan glanced down and saw a thin strip of plastic securing the Iranian's wrists. Taking out another, wider flex cuff, Bolan stooped down and crisscrossed a second band over the first. He then did a quick but thorough search of the man's pockets and body and lifted the prone Iranian back into the rear of the van. The distant, alternating blast of police sirens echoed in the night.

Bolan scooped the weapons out of the van and tossed them on the ground.

"Let's get out of here," he said, slamming the rear doors. "Unless you want to stick around and answer twenty questions for the police."

Crissey smiled and began trotting back toward his car. Bolan moved to the front of the van, pulled out the last two bodies and threw them into the alley. He did a quick survey of the scene. There were enough bodies, weapons and expended rounds to keep the police busy for a while. The thing to do now was vacate the area and hope no one noticed all the bullet holes in the van.

"I say," Crissey said, pausing at the side of his vehicle. "Shouldn't we at least move those chaps off to the side?"

"Not unless you want to do it with an audience," Bolan said, slipping behind the wheel. The interior was slick with blood, but he had no time to clean it off. Instead he cocked his feet back and kicked the corners of the damaged windshield. The glass cracked and bulged, then separated from the frame, coming out in one piece. Instead of dropping it to the ground, Bolan pulled the glass back inside and set it in the rear section. There was no sense in leaving a clue as to what type of vehicle they might be driving or what condition it was in. "I'll follow you to your embassy, then we can see what we've got."

"Righto." Crissey grinned. "And don't forget we drive on the proper side of the roadway here in Hong Kong. The left side."

"I'll do my best to remember," Bolan said. "Hopefully none of the cops will stop me for driving without a windshield."

Crissey looked around at the four bodies and scattered weapons.

"Perhaps," he said, "they'll be a bit busy sorting this one out."

THE MANTIS HAD finished stuffing the money into a makeshift sack he'd fashioned from the overcoat. He was calling Master Chen when he heard the sound. The slight creak of the rear door being opened. Another of Chong's hired assassins?

"Your voice hesitates," Master Chen said. "Is something wrong?"

"Trouble," the Mantis whispered. "I will meet your men at the rendezvous point."

He terminated the call and slipped the cell phone back into his pocket as he dropped the package and melted into the shadows to survey the scene. He didn't have to wait long. Two men emerged from the corridor and into the circle of light, their arms extended and holding small, semiautomatic pistols. One of the pistols had a shiny, chrome-like finish, sparkling like a jewel in the garish light.

"Hello," the first one said. "Look at those chaps."

English, the Mantis thought. MI6? Regardless, they were both careless men with not long to live.

"Looks like there's been a bit of a row," the second added. He moved toward the bundled overcoat and kicked it. "We'd better look into this."

"Right," the first one said. "But let's back off and call for assistance. We need to clear this place and that's going to be a bit of a chore."

The last thing the Mantis needed was a squad of British agents nosing around. The discovery of the bodies was both inevitable and desirable—the price of betrayal had to be shown—just not at this time. He felt in his vest for another dart. He would only need one. He gripped it tightly in his right hand. One of the Brits holstered his gun and took out a cell phone. The other stood holding his weapon down by his leg, the bright slide once again reflecting the overhead lighting. The Englishman squatted down next to the bundled overcoat and began untying it.

"Let's see what we've got here," he said.

"Better to wait on that," his partner replied. The

Mantis threw his first dart. It caught the man in the throat. He dropped the cell phone and grabbed at his neck. The other one quickly whirled, extending his pistol as he rose to a crouch. The Mantis was already running forward, leaping upward, his right leg cocked back. At the apex of his leap he snapped his foot outward, catching the second agent under the jaw. The man's head jerked up and back, then his whole body bobbled drunkenly as he collapsed onto his stomach. The Mantis landed on the man's back, using the edge of his foot in a downward stomp to assure that the neck was indeed broken. Satisfied that it was, he whirled, caught the staggering first man with an arcing hook kick. This one fell as if he'd been poleaxed.

The Mantis retrieved his dart, wiped the blood on the dead man's jacket and replaced the dart in his vest. The shiny Walther PPS lay a few inches from the second agent's fingers. The Mantis picked it up. Some fancy English letters, *TNT,* were engraved on the slide. He would give Chong's .380 to the master, but why not take something for himself? It would make a nice souvenir. He pocketed the pistol, grabbed the bundled overcoat and took out his cell phone.

Master Chen answered after the first ring. "All is well?"

"All is well," the Mantis said.

"It grieves me that you encountered unexpected trouble."

"It was nothing," the Mantis said as he surveyed the scene with satisfaction, "that I could not handle."

BY THE TIME they got close to the British embassy, Bolan's eyes were stinging from driving the truck with no windshield. His cell phone rang and he glanced at the screen: Crissey.

"Turn left at the next corner, will you?" the Englishman said. "I've got a couple blokes standing by with a truck so none of our omnipresent embassy watchers see us bringing that wretched van inside."

Bolan watched as Crissey's car made the quick left turn. Pulling in after him, Bolan found himself on a semidark side street. Ahead he saw a parked truck with Chinese lettering on the side and an open back end. He parked next to the truck and got out. Three men rushed over to the van and began removing the crate. He gave them a hand, and in about sixty seconds they had it transferred to the new truck. They took the trussed-up prisoner next. The man was still unconscious but would hopefully awaken and give them some good intel. If not, Bolan was sure Stony Man could put the guy on ice somewhere.

Crissey had been standing a few feet away holding his cell phone to his ear. He turned to the three new men. "Would one of you be so kind as to dump the van down the way?" he said. "And do take our friend and his little package to the designated drop point at your leisure."

The other men nodded and hurried away.

Bolan watched as the truck with the prisoner and the crate drove off down the street, followed by the damaged van. He figured the Brits were perfectly capable of getting whatever was in the crate to a safe location for further review as well as interrogating the prisoner. The Agency could tag up with them later and decide if the Iranians had bought the real deal or not.

Bolan looked at Crissey, who still stood holding

his cell phone with a worried expression on his face. "What's up?"

Crissey heaved a sigh. "We've lost contact with two of my men—the ones who followed the Chinese with the briefcase." He bit his lower lip. "They haven't called in and I can't seem to raise them."

"Let's go find them," Bolan said, heading for the Englishman's car.

Crissey nodded and hurried to the driver's side. As Crissey drove to the warehouse district where they'd left the other two agents, Bolan felt his satellite phone vibrate. He took it out, glanced at the screen and answered the call with "Don't you ever sleep?"

Brognola's deep chuckle came from the other side of the world. "Hell, it's zero-eight-fifteen here. Time for my midmorning snack while I get ready to watch *Let's Make a Deal*."

"Why don't I like the sound of that?" Bolan asked.

"You must be psychic." Brognola's laugh came through clear as a bell. "I need to run something by you, but how did the mission go?"

Just then Crissey pulled past the empty car the two MI6 agents had been driving.

"Hal, hold on," Bolan said. He reached for his Beretta with his other hand.

No one else was in sight. Crissey swung the car into the alleyway and proceeded slowly down the narrow route.

"Striker, you still there?" Brognola asked.

The headlights shone over a pair of legs extending out from behind a row of garbage cans.

"Bloody hell," Crissey said.

"Let me call you back," Bolan said into the phone.

2

It was almost four in the morning by the time Bolan and Crissey transported the two dead agents, Thomas Norris Trent and Peter J. Helmsworth, back to the British Embassy. Searching and clearing the rest of the warehouse had been tedious, but necessary, as well as erasing any trace that MI6 had been involved. Not finding Trent's weapon had drawn the process out further, and finally the threat of a nascent sun forced them to abandon their search. They left the rest of the mess for the Hong Kong police. When they finally sat down in a small room next to the embassy cafeteria, neither man had much appetite, but both needed a cup of strong coffee. They'd been up for more than twenty-four hours straight. The Brit was holding up pretty well, Bolan observed, maintaining a bit of the traditional stiff upper lip, but the Executioner could tell the man was deeply affected by the deaths.

"Did you know those men well?" he asked, taking a sip from his mug.

Crissey nodded. "Tom Trent and I have been here on assignment for the past year and a half. Before that we did a tour in Afghanistan." He forced a smile and dumped some more sugar into his cup. "After that one, we thought coming here would be a bit of a vacation."

Bolan said nothing. He knew that dropping your guard on any assignment, no matter how benign it looked, could be a fatal error. "At least they'll be buried in home soil."

Crissey nodded again. "I do wish we could have found Trent's pistol. I would have liked his father to have it. It was a stainless steel Walther PPS. Quite the good gun. Had *TNT* engraved on the slide in fancy script." Crissey smiled wistfully. "His initials. Made quite a joke of it."

"Think his killer took it?" Bolan asked.

Crissey shrugged. "Most likely, but perhaps that's preferable to the Chinese finding it and being able to trace it back to us." His brow furrowed. "Trent was no neophyte. He knew his stuff."

Bolan considered this. Trent had apparently had his neck broken. There was also a large dark spot on the right side of the dead man's jaw, although Bolan hadn't taken the time to examine it closely. At least it appeared Trent's death had been quick—no needless suffering.

Bolan drank some more coffee and stood. "I have to make a call."

"Certainly," Crissey said, also standing. "I'd better check in myself." He showed Bolan to an adjacent room and left.

Bolan punched in the digits of Hal Brognola's number on the satellite phone. He answered on the second ring, sounding as gruff as ever. "About damn time you called back. What, you enjoying the Hong Kong nightlife, or something?"

"Not hardly," Bolan said. "I was helping our friends at MI6 clean up a little mess. They lost a couple guys."

"Oh," Brognola said. "Sorry to hear that." He waited a beat, then asked, "You get the package?"

"The Brits are giving it a once-over now, along with a prisoner."

Brognola grunted an approval. "One of the buyers?"

"Affirmative," Bolan said. "And he speaks Farsi."

Brognola swore. "That's not good. If the Chinese are exporting technology to Iran it could mean big trouble."

"For what it's worth, I don't think the Chinese government's involved. If they were, I doubt they'd be using a channel like the Triads."

"True," Brognola said. "But it no doubt points to some high level corruption in the PLA."

Bolan had considered that possibility, as well. Corruption was rampant in China, especially in the government. Having access to the guidance system for an advanced missile would mean somebody who was pretty high up the food chain was complicit.

"Anyway," Brognola said, clearing his throat. "I'm glad you intercepted it. Good work. So how you doing?"

Bolan smiled in spite of his fatigue. The sound of Brognola shifting gears meant the other shoe was about to drop. "I could use a couple hours' sleep, but what have you got?"

Brognola laughed, but it sounded forced. "Can't put nothing over on you, can I?" He cleared his throat again. "Since you got that one about wrapped up, you feel up to another mission?"

Bolan paused as he felt exhaustion seeping through him.

Brognola seemed to take his hesitation as reticence. "I mean, since you're in the neighborhood and all."

"Can the Mr. Rogers imitation. What've you got?"

Brognola sighed. "You ever hear of a Chinese dissident called Han, Son Chu, aka Sammo Han?"

"Sammo Han," Bolan said. "Isn't he that one-armed lawyer?"

"Lawyer, activist, blogging sensation and darling of the free press."

"Free press?" Bolan said with a chuckle. "In China?"

"The world press, as well. Anyway, he was placed under house arrest two days ago." Brognola paused and then emitted what sounded like a grunt of pain or pleasure. Bolan imagined him taking a long sip of some of Aaron "The Bear" Kurtzman's god-awful coffee. Bolan drank some of his own coffee and found it weak by comparison.

"Anyway, seems that Sammo Han's not only a celebrity on the world stage, he's also valuable to the USA. But word is, the People's Standing Committee is set to charge him with sedition, lock him up and throw away the key."

"After they give him a fair trial, you mean."

"If he even gets to a trial. Most likely he'll be conveniently killed trying to resist arrest. That Agency team was sent to do an emergency evac from Beijing for him and his family."

Which was why, Bolan thought, they had no one to follow up on the Iranian/Triad deal, and I had to fill in. "This Sammo Han must have some very valuable intel."

"Well," Brognola continued, "everything was set until the team leader, Wayne Tressman, got pinched. He's in a Chinese prison in Song Jing. Just outside the capital."

Bolan frowned and thought about the unpleasant prospects of an American intelligence officer being in the custody of the Chinese.

"Any progress through diplomatic channels?"

"So far, the Chinese aren't even acknowledging that

they have him," Brognola said. "The rest of the team's still in place, but they're kind of green and they haven't made a move yet. I need somebody I can count on to go there and give me a sitrep. Interested?"

Bolan blew out a slow breath. "We talking about a jail break?"

"If the diplomats fail."

Bolan sighed. "When do they ever succeed?"

Brognola barked another laugh. Two forced laughs in a single conversation. This was getting serious.

"All right," Bolan said. "When do I leave for Beijing?"

"Aaron's got you on a flight leaving in four hours."

"Pretty sure I was going to say yes, weren't you?"

Brognola snorted. "Let's just say I had a real strong hunch."

"Yeah, well if you get any new hunches about the Powerball jackpot," Bolan said, "buy an extra ticket for me."

"Hey, that's not all."

"You've got more good news?"

"Sure do," Brognola said. "I've got help on the way."

"Who?"

"Grimaldi."

"Jack?" It was Bolan's turn to chuckle. "I thought you said you were sending help? Talk about importing a bull into a China shop."

"Well, he won't get there for a while. He's traveling commercial."

"I pity the pilots."

"So do I," Brognola said. "You two will be there as sports journalists covering the World Asia Track and Field Games, not to mention that boxing match a couple of days later. The Chinese world champion is making his professional debut in Shanghai. That should give you guys the run of the place, not to mention a chance to see the fight."

"Well, for the record," Bolan said, "I'd settle for a couple cold ones in front of a big flat screen in Vegas."

Brognola barked a final laugh before his voice took on a more serious tone. "Hey, Striker."

"Yeah?"

"Thanks for never letting me down."

Beijing

GENERAL WONG SU TONG of the People's Liberation Army stepped out of the jeep and told the underling to wait for him. He was perhaps one block from the entrance to the Forbidden City. The general carried himself with his customary military bearing, proud of the image he projected: a well-built man with the aplomb and power of a professional solider. He worked hard to maintain his sleek, iron physique—despite being in his early fifties—and kept his hair dyed jet-black. A solemn yet serene expression was on his face, even though the icy fingers of incipient and nagging panic were pinching their way up and down his spine.

He hated these subterfuges, these clandestine meetings that Chen insisted upon, but he also understood their necessity. Wong was no stranger to treachery. He knew full well that despite his exalted position in the Central Military Committee, spies were watching his every move. Several members of the all-powerful Standing Committee, who smiled to his face, would love to stick a knife between his ribs if the opportunity presented itself. And if they ever found evidence of his covert dealings, those knives would appear quickly. If

he were caught, if his secret dealings with the Triads
and his hidden assets were discovered, Wong would be
arrested immediately. And no doubt his trial would be
both expedient and lethal.

He walked briskly past the throngs of tourists and
made his way to the whispering wall. More tourists,
some Americans or Europeans, but mostly Chinese,
strolled by. No one dared look him in the eye. A group
of soldiers passed and saluted. Wong suddenly regretted
he hadn't changed to civilian clothes. His uniform made
him stand out like a tiger in a marketplace. But time
was of the essence. He paused under the entranceway
to the Forbidden City, underneath the massive banner
of Mao, and glanced around again. No sign of Chen.

Where was the son of a whore?

The past week had been a disaster. The deal with the
Iranians, the stolen payoff money, the missing guidance
system and, most of all, the loss of his personal flash
drive, the dragon key. His whole life, as well as his fu-
ture, was on that device. It contained all the bank account numbers and passwords to his secret accounts in
Hong Kong and Zurich, the special accounts his brother-
in-law, Yoon, had set up for him. The accounts that assured he would be richer than he ever imagined when
he eventually left the PLA, and China, for good.

He silently cursed the woman who'd stolen it from
him, and his own stupidity for being so drunk and in-
fatuated with her red-haired beauty that he hadn't immediately caught the substitution. But she had been so
very talented, and the copy was so exact…

The fingers of his right hand momentarily went to
the chain around his neck, the chain that always held the
flash drive, disguised as a dragon's head. Now it held
the ersatz dragon key—the one the Russian had sub-

stituted. How had she known about it, much less taken the real one and replaced it with an exact duplicate?

Although the device was protected with a password, there was a slight possibility that someone might eventually breach the code. The Politburo Standing Committee would certainly have people who could do it. So would the Americans. He wondered which would be worse. The Americans would no doubt blackmail him, but the Committee would publically rend him limb from limb.

"General," a soft voice said.

Wong looked around, but saw no one except the pretty Chinese girl smiling at him on the opposite side of the nearest obelisk. He could barely hear her above the cacophony of the milling crowd.

"General," the girl said again.

Wong squinted at her and raised an eyebrow.

"The man you seek awaits inside the Hall of Eternal Harmony."

She had to be one of Chen's girls, Wong thought. He took another moment to appraise her. Her dark hair was long and fell like a curtain over part of her face. It was a pretty face, and although she wore pants and a loose-fitting shirt, Wong could tell her figure was excellent. The old, fat Triad leader liked to send young, fetching creatures to do his bidding. The general had no doubt she could most likely slice a man's throat as soon as seduce him. He tugged the corner of his mouth into a slight smile, nodded to her and went to meet Chen. An interior meeting was eminently preferable to outside, where the prying eyes of the Committee could be hiding among the throngs of tourists.

He strode through the gate, bypassing a line of people at the ticket booth. A guard saw him and immedi-

ately came to attention as Wong walked past. Inside, the
Forbidden City was divided into a complex of beautiful
courtyards and ceremonial halls.

Wong stopped at the entrance to the Hall of Eternal Harmony and shook a cigarette out of his pack. He
lighted it and drew deeply as he glanced around. The
girl who had whispered to him was walking about thirty
meters behind with two men, both dressed in loose-
fitting jackets. Obviously they were Chen's security
team. He never went anywhere without one, and Wong
could hardly blame him.

The son of a whore is cautious and thorough, he
thought.

Wong took a few more drags on the cigarette, waiting for Chen's trio to get nearer. When they were about
five meters away, Wong crushed the butt under his shoe.
The security team would no doubt keep any intrud-
ing eyes—and cameras—away from the meeting. He
smiled slightly at the girl as the three grew closer, then
Wong went into the courtyard. She was indeed a rare
beauty.

He walked past a fountain with two stone dragons
flanked by tigers. The tigers, his zodiac animal, buoyed
his spirits slightly. Chen, Wong knew, had been born
under the sign of the rat, which meant he was skilled at
survival, subterfuge and gathering money.

Wong passed by a series of trellises replete with
winding stems of blossoms and caught sight of Chen,
who was sitting on a bench in front of a row of cypress
trees, holding a flower.

He looked more like someone's benevolent grand-
father than the merciless leader of the Sun Yang Triad,
the largest and most powerful of the Chinese crime
gangs. Chen had survived the Cultural Revolution, a

forced exile in Hong Kong, the internal power struggles of the Triad and innumerable attempts on his life. But then again, he was a rat, and rats were nothing if not resourceful.

Chen's mouth flickered into a smile, and he bowed his head slightly as Wong approached. Wong did the same and sat on the opposite end of the bench. They were close enough to hear each other's words, but they wouldn't look like acquaintances.

They sat in silence for perhaps half a minute. Wong was growing impatient when Chen finally broke the silence. "Is it not miraculous, the way the leaves turn toward the sunlight? Do you ever wonder if they can feel the warmth?" Chen laughed softly, his chuckle sounding like the flow of water over pebbles in a brook.

Wong had little time for the riddles of horticulture. "Have you found out anything?"

Chen's laugh came again, but this time it reminded Wong of an erosive leak down a wall. Wong's face twisted into an expression of displeasure as he turned toward the Triad boss.

"I asked if you had found anything."

Chen turned his head so they were now face-to-face. "Of course I have, Comrade General."

He turned back, folded his hands over his belly and sat there like a smiling Buddha.

"Chen, I don't have time for your games. Tell me what you've learned."

Chen continued to sit in silence, a peaceful smile gracing his lips as he twirled the flower in his hand. Just as Wong felt himself ready to explode, the other man spoke. "Do not worry. As the farmer plows the earth, its destruction lays the seeds for a new beginning."

Another damn riddle. Wong made no attempt to hide

his growing anger. "Damn you. Are you going to tell me or not?"

The older man's smile did not alter. He raised an eyebrow and stared at the general for several seconds more. "Did they not teach you the value of patience in the military academy?"

Wong felt like wringing the old bastard's neck. He shot a look at the guards—the two males facing outward, the female watching them. Wong considered the risk of giving Chen a hard slap, but the bodyguards would be on him in seconds, general or not. Thus, he refrained and snorted in disgust. "We shouldn't be wasting time here. Someone might see us together."

"Did I not say all was well?" Chen said. "My favorite disciple, Lee Son Yin, has watchful eyes. We are safe."

"What about my money?"

"It has been recovered. It will soon be in my hands." He paused. "And will be deposited in your special account, when the time comes."

"And the dragon key?" Wong asked, trying not to sound too eager. Without the flash drive no deposits or withdrawals could be made.

"Some matters are more quickly resolved than others."

So Chen didn't have it. Wong swallowed hard and thought about this. "Do you know who arranged the theft? Who paid that woman?"

"I have my number one man working toward this discovery," Chen said. "And its resolution."

For a moment Wong wondered if Chen himself was behind the theft. The Triads controlled everything, including the prostitution rings, and had been arranging his Hong Kong liaisons for the past several years. But this was the first time something like this had happened.

Surely, if Chen had planned a betrayal, he would have acted before this. Or would he?

"And the missile guidance system," Wong said. "What about that?"

Chen sighed. "It is in the possession of the British and the Americans."

"Americans?" Wong said. "We've just captured an American. A spy. He is being interrogated now."

Chen nodded. "A fact of which I am well aware."

Wong blew out a long breath and reached for his cigarettes. After sticking one between his lips and holding the lighter to it, he turned back to Chen. "What did you find out from that Russian whore?"

"In life, there is sometimes a certain unavoidable unpleasantness. Learn to dismiss it, as the water in the pond rolls off the back of the swimming duck."

More platitudes, Wong thought. "Did she tell you who paid her to steal the dragon key?"

"She gave us the name," Chen said.

Wong felt more than ever like lashing out, knocking the old fool to the ground, but he knew better. "Who?" he asked. "I'll track him down and kill him myself."

"That is not advisable."

"What? Why not?"

Chen smelled the blossom. "Is it not a shame that our country's recent economic progress has so poisoned our air, our land, our water?"

Wong was at the end of his patience. "I asked you a question. Who is he?"

When Chen did not answer immediately, Wong emitted a growl. "I'm waiting. And no more damn riddles, understand?"

Chen smiled and put his palms together in a prayer-like gesture, cupping the blossom in between. "I have offended you, and for that I am truly sorry. But as I said before, a wise man must not lose sight of his goal, lest he act with impetuousness."

Wong drew deeply on the cigarette. What was Chen getting at?

As if he could sense the unasked question, Chen said, "The man who engineered the theft is familiar to you."

Wong blew twin plumes of smoke out his nostrils. "His name. Give me his damn name. I'll get it out of him."

Chen's smile did not lose its beatific grace. He shook his head fractionally. "Once again, remember that patience is the supreme virtue. It should first be considered that if something happens to this man, the dragon key could be lost forever, or delivered into the wrong hands."

"I promise not to act with rashness," Wong said. "But I need to know who he is. I need to know the name of the man who holds the knife to my balls."

"As well you should," Chen said. "Just give me your word you will take no action without first obtaining clearance from me."

Chen held the ultimate trump card, but Wong still needed to formulate his own plan, just in case the Triad boss betrayed him. "I give you my word as an officer and general of the People's Liberation Army."

The smile vanished and Chen's dark eyes shot toward him, staring from beneath their heavy lids.

"I repeat, the man who betrayed you must not yet be contacted or harmed," he said. "Do you understand me?"

The Triad leader's tone left no question as to who was in command. It was not a request. Wong suddenly realized that up until now Chen had been toying with him, allowing him to believe he was in charge. Now it was brutally apparent that the Triad boss controlled Wong's fate. The general had little choice but to acquiesce.

"Yes," Wong said. "He will not be contacted or harmed without your approval."

Chen's face softened into a smile. "Excellent. When men strive to overcome adversity, they must not work at cross-purposes."

Wong was sick of the aphorisms, but he held his tongue for the time being.

"The man has been a thorn in your side," Chen said. "And a problem for the Standing Committee, as well."

Wong furrowed his brow in concentration, then suddenly he knew. "Han Son Chu?"

Chen smiled and nodded. "You see, oftentimes the answer you seek lies within your own knowledge."

Han Son Chu, Wong thought. Sammo Han to the Western press. But how did he trace me to that Russian whore? And how did he know about the dragon key? Wong did some mental calculations. The time frame did fit. The one-armed bastard must have followed him to Hong Kong and somehow bribed the whore to steal it. No matter. Han was under house detention. It would be simple to grab him and reobtain the dragon key.

"Is this blossom not beautiful?" Chen held the flower toward Wong. "But just as the rose on the vine is lovely, one must be careful to avoid the accompanying thorns."

Another riddle, Wong thought. He took one last drag on his cigarette and ground it under the sole of his shoe.

"The Committee is getting ready to move against Han as we speak," Wong said. "He's already under house detention, but if he's arrested and brought to trial for his disruptive activities, he could bring up my indiscretions in a public forum. And then our involvement will surely come to light. We're both on the line here."

Chen nodded. "But even the Committee would not move in such drastic fashion at this time," he said. "The world press is swarming Beijing, and reporters are following the American movie star who is seeking an audience with Han. The last thing the Committee would want is for China to lose face on the world stage."

Wong nodded. "This gives us time to confront the bastard privately. Get the dragon key back before they initiate a complete arrest."

Chen shook his head. "Regrettably, there is more. The American spy you mentioned…"

Wong frowned. "What about him?"

"He is being held at Song Jing Prison, is he not?"

"Yes. How did you know that?"

Chen's smile returned, as placid as ever. "I have my sources."

Wong's frown deepened. Was there nothing this old bastard didn't know?

Chen waited a beat and continued, "The interrogation of the American has yielded a bit of information concerning Han. He is getting ready to defect."

"That one-armed son of a whore," Wong said. "I'll take pleasure in watching him die slowly."

"Most assuredly. But let us assume Han anticipated his arrest. Would he not keep the device in a secret place? Would he not make arrangements to release it to a confederate if he dies prior to its recovery? We must fully consider this risk, should it fall into the wrong hands."

Like those of the Standing Committee, Wong thought.

"Thus," Chen said, "we must move with circumspection."

This did nothing to ease the growing tension in Wong's gut.

"Do you understand?" Chen asked.

"Yes." Wong took another cigarette out of his pack. "What do you want me to do?"

Chen smiled at his acquiescence. "For the moment you can do nothing but stand and await my further instructions. But do not despair. I have a plan in mind, but it will require your assistance." He heard Chen's soft chuckle again. "As I said, be patient and trust in me. It shall all be resolved in an expeditious manner, Comrade General. Trust in your humble servant."

Humble servant. The old liar. Wong forced himself to nod in agreement, and then he lit his cigarette.

3

During the flight from Hong Kong to Beijing, Bolan took a combat nap. He was awakened by a pretty flight attendant who advised him to fasten his seat belt and prepare for landing.

"Welcome to Beijing," she said.

As Bolan looked around and assessed his surroundings, the businessman next to him flashed a nervous smile. He was in his mid-to-late fifties.

"American?" the man asked.

Bolan nodded.

"You a soldier once?" he said, giving Bolan a thorough look.

"Once," Bolan replied.

"Me, too," the man said. "I was PLA artillery in our last war. With the Vietnamese."

"I heard it was short but bloody," Bolan said.

The man nodded. "Very much blood. Hard fighting, but we won." He smiled. "War is cruel and sometimes strange. Back then I destroyed things. Now I build them. I have my own construction company. There is a building boom here in China."

At the expense of the rural poor, Bolan thought. Or so he'd heard. Maybe he'd get a chance to see firsthand.

The plane began a slow descent, and Bolan glanced

out the window. They were perhaps a thousand feet up now. Row after row of buildings and houses extended in every direction below, an ever-growing sea of humanity. "Looks like the construction business is good," he said.

"Business is business." The man smiled. "Always number one when China number one."

Bolan nodded politely and braced himself as the pilot sent the plane down the runway with a hard initial bounce followed by several more. The flaps and brakes kicked in, slowing the craft into a noisy deceleration.

Welcome to Beijing, Bolan thought.

THE MANTIS SAT in the back of a Mercedes limo as the driver headed to a commercial district—a busy area filled with restaurants, tea parlors and bars. The trip from Hong Kong to Beijing had been comfortable on Master Chen's private jet, but the Mantis had never let the suitcase or the small newspaper-wrapped package out of his sight.

Avoiding the cluster of humanity slowing the commercial airlines was one of the amenities Master Chen's top enforcer enjoyed. The waiting limousine at the airport had been another. It amused him, however, that a man as powerful as the master would choose to meet in this district of low-grade restaurants. Pedestrians and bicyclists cluttered the roadway before them, and the driver continually blew his horn. The people scattered like unruly chickens.

The Mantis sat back in the comfortable seat and waited, practicing his mental concentration by seeking serenity.

His *sifu*'s words came back to him: Strive for harmony in all things, and embrace moments of solitude, for the march of time and life is often cruel and unforgiving.

Unforgiving… Just like Master Chen. The Mantis traced his fingers over the tightly wrapped package. He'd tied the twine himself, feeling a slight twinge of regret over its contents. But, as his *sifu* had said, life is often cruel.

Finally, the Mantis felt the vehicle slowing to a stop. The screen was down, and through the windshield he could see the endless rows of glowing, twisted neon spelling out Chinese characters. He pushed open the door and got out, surveying the scene in both directions. A sea of people moved along the street in the late afternoon, but the Mantis saw nothing out of the ordinary. No sign of police, uniformed or not. Even so, he slipped the package into his jacket pocket, grabbed the suitcase and slammed the car door behind him. He strode to the next corner and turned as the limousine lurched into the street again.

The Mantis walked half a block down, crossed the street then paused to see if anyone followed. Satisfied that no one was watching him, he walked to the next juncture, an alleyway that led behind the row of buildings. He turned down the alley and went to the third door, which opened as he approached. No doubt the limo driver had used his cell phone to alert those inside.

The Mantis stepped into a storage room, pausing to let his eyes adjust to the low lighting while readying his unencumbered left hand into a stiffened, spear-like weapon. Even though he trusted there would be no waiting ambush, he always remained at the ready.

Two men motioned him forward. "Come this way," the taller one said, holding back a beaded curtain. The Mantis stepped through the opening and saw another lackey holding open the door to the adjacent room. After the Mantis stepped through, the door slid closed behind him.

Master Chen sat on the floor, a large table in front of him cluttered with plates of food. He used chopsticks to pick up a bit of rice inside a green leaf, dipped it into some sauce and jammed it into his waiting mouth. As he chewed, he held up his hand and waggled his fingers in the customary gesture for the Mantis to approach.

The Mantis bowed and set the suitcase next to Chen. He reached into his pocket and set the wrapped package on top of the valise.

Master Chen looked at it and smiled. "Sit, Lee."

A place had been set for him at the opposite end of the small table. The Mantis sat and pulled the chopsticks from their wrapping paper. Chen plucked a few more morsels from the expanse of food in front of them.

"Your trip to Hong Kong was indeed fruitful," he said. "Am I to assume you achieved all that I asked of you?"

The Mantis nodded.

"Good, good," Chen said, shifting some food in his mouth. He chewed some more, then smiled, showing bits of food stuck along his gum line and around his front teeth. "Are you not hungry from your long journey?"

The Mantis reached over and grabbed a small bowl, shoveling rice and vegetables into it. He ate one bite, so as not to offend Master Chen, then set the chopsticks down.

The Triad master grabbed two slices of sweet-and sour pork and shoved them into his mouth before speaking. "The general will be pleased that his money was recovered." Chen's brow furrowed. "And those who betrayed us have been adequately punished?"

"I dropped the Russian girl's body in the harbor," the Mantis said. "The others I left in the warehouse."

Master Chen's lips flickered into a tiny smile as he glanced toward the tightly wrapped newspaper package. "Chong's treachery upset me greatly. I remember when you and he were boys. For him to devise such an elaborate deception, and think he could steal from me, is like a cloud passing in front of the sun."

The Mantis said nothing.

"You did as I instructed?" Chen asked.

"Just as you instructed, Master," the Mantis said.

The other man's smile widened. He set his chopsticks down and reached over for the newspaper wrapping. After brushing away the bowls and cups in front of him, he set the package on the table and pulled at the knotted string. Master Chen frowned, then looked over at the Mantis.

"A gift should not be like a puzzle box," he said.

"Forgive me," the Mantis replied. In one smooth gesture he swept the *balisong* knife from his pocket and opened it. The Mantis rose to his knees and slid the sharpened edge of the blade under the string, cutting the knot with a quick flick of his wrist. He receded back to his sitting position and swung the *balisong* closed.

Master Chen acknowledged the act with a slight bow. Then he unwound the string and carefully opened the folded paper. Inside was a clear plastic bag that contained three severed fingers: index, middle and ring. The master smiled and looked at the Mantis. "A traitor's final gesture of fidelity to the Triad." The smile faded as he leaned forward. "Tell me, did you make him suffer before he died?"

The Mantis nodded, not mentioning that following those instructions had almost caused him to get caught by the British agents. Luckily, he had not allowed his former friendship with Chong or the unpleasantness of the task to distract him from his eternal vigilance.

The master took another look at the fingers, then rewrapped them in the newspaper and pushed the package aside. He reached for his chopsticks again.

"There is another pressing matter," he said as he snared some more pork. "It involves the recovery of the general's dragon key."

The Mantis nodded. "You wish me to obtain it from Han Son Chu?"

Chen chewed thoughtfully, then nodded. He held up his chopsticks. "But it is a most delicate matter. Perhaps Son Yin may be of assistance."

At the mention of his sister's name, the Mantis felt his throat tighten. But still, Chen owned both of them, as surely as he owned a treasure trove of riches and all the other men and women who worked under him.

He was the master.

The Mantis bowed his head. "She is well?"

Chen's beatific smile returned. "She is, and so shall she remain." He snapped his fingers and the sliding door on the other side of the room pushed open.

Lee Son Yin, the sister of the Mantis, entered wearing a long silk gown.

EXPERIENCE HAD TAUGHT Bolan to travel light. One ditty bag containing a change of clothes and a few toiletries was all he had with him as he stepped off the plane. Whatever else he needed in the way of weaponry would have to wait until it was channeled through diplomatic means to the American Embassy. Bolan also had little

trouble spotting the agent who was supposed to meet
him in the massive Beijing airport. The woman stood
by a section of stainless steel pillars that stretched upward into an archway. She looked Chinese, but something about her said Made in the USA. Perhaps it was
that air of confidence in her walk as she rolled her suitcase through the huge lobby.

"You must be Matt Cooper, right?" she said.

Bolan nodded, trying to place her American accent,
if any. California was his best guess. She was about
five-six, wore large glasses and had her hair in a long
braid. Her blouse and pants seemed to conceal an ath-
letic frame.

"I'm Kelly Yang," she said. "It'll be less conspicuous if we don't walk together, so keep going, okay?"

"Sounds good." Bolan kept walking toward the exit.

Yang waited and then turned in front of him and
began heading for the main exit, as well.

Bolan humored her by staying a few feet behind her.

As they got to the doors, the young woman turned
left and began heading toward a long line of taxis. Bolan
followed her as they walked past cab after cab, the driv-
ers whistling and yelling to attract fares.

They neared the end and Yang turned and winked.
"Hey, big guy, want to share a ride?"

A blue van pulled up with Chinese characters on
the side. *China Gates* and *Number One Tourist Service*
were stenciled in English along the top. Two Asian men
sat in the front seats. The driver seemed to be around
forty with a cigarette dangling from his lips. The passenger was younger and had a clean-cut look about him.
He hopped out and slid open the side door of the van,
taking Yang's suitcase, and then turning to Bolan.

"Taxi, mister? We offer the best service in Beijing."

Bolan held out his bag and let the young guy take it. The kid appeared to be in his early twenties, about the same as Agent Yang. Brognola hadn't been exaggerating when he'd said the Agency's team was a little green. Bolan got inside and the agent slammed the door behind him. As soon as he got back in, the van took off, shooting by several taxis and limos with a loud blare of its horn.

"Easy, Herbie," the young guy said. "We definitely don't want to get stopped by the cops."

"No problem," Herbie said, hitting himself on the chest with his right hand. "Number one driver."

The young guy turned and extended his hand toward Bolan. "I'm Peter Huang, Mr. Cooper. We got word via the embassy to expect you."

"Yeah, a few hours ago," Yang said.

"Sorry," Bolan replied. "China Air was running a bit behind today."

"When doesn't it?" Yang said. She took off the glasses. "These are just for show. Meet Herbie Zheng, our number one driver and asset in Beijing."

Herbie twisted in the seat and flashed a smile, the cigarette still dangling from his mouth.

"We also got word that we're to defer to you regarding the op," Huang said, still twisted around in the seat to face Bolan. "What are your orders, sir?"

"First," Bolan said, "you can quit calling me sir. Are both of you fluent in Mandarin?"

"We are," Huang said.

"I speak Cantonese, too," Yang added. "And Korean and Vietnamese."

"That could come in handy," Bolan replied. "What's the situation with Tressman?"

Huang grimaced. "Wayne's still in Song Jing. We're

under orders not to try to see him, and we have it on good authority that he's still alive." He looked down. "They were working him over pretty good, and then stopped."

"Where did you get that information?" Bolan asked.

Huang gestured toward the driver. "Herbie has a contact in the prison. He's been feeding us bits of info."

"Number one info," Herbie said. "Me number one agent." He grinned and puffed on the cigarette. "Worth lotsa money."

"Any word as to why they supposedly backed off on the beatings?" Bolan asked.

"Who knows?" Huang shot back. "This is China. You think they're gonna follow our rules?"

"I hate to think of Wayne being beaten," Yang said. Her voice sounded brittle.

The tension was obviously getting to both of these greenhorns.

"Let's stay on point." Bolan had his work cut out for him with this group. Sending a couple of inexperienced kids on a mission like this showed questionable judgment from the get-go. But for now he had to play the hand he'd been dealt. "How many hours has he been in custody?"

Huang looked at the roof of the van and blew out a short breath. "Fourteen."

"They haven't even notified the American Embassy of his arrest," Yang said.

"Like I told you," Huang said, "this is China."

"All right," Bolan said. "Let's assume he's given up at least some of the information on your mission. What could he have told them?"

Huang sighed and rubbed his temples. "We were sent

here to evacuate an asset and his family. A dissident lawyer named Han Son Chu."

"Sammo Han," Herbie said. He looked in the rear-view mirror and grinned. "Everybody like him. He's famous."

"So I heard," Bolan said. "When and how did Tressman get arrested?"

"Wayne and I were in Han's house," Huang said. "Yang was out in front watching. We were going over our evac plan when all of a sudden this police van shows up. Wayne sent me out the back way. He stayed. We thought they were there to intimidate Han. I'd just made it out when I heard the police yelling inside." He looked down. "I shouldn't have left him alone."

"Then you'd both be in prison now," Bolan said. "And we'd have two people to break out instead of one."

"They took Wayne away in the van and left a couple guards by the house." Huang compressed his lips. He almost looked ready to cry. "Han and his family are under house detention, being investigated for disruptive activities."

"Are you still in contact with them?" Bolan asked.

Huang nodded.

"How do you do that?"

"They let Mrs. Han go out to the market," Yang said. "That's how we've been communicating."

Bolan considered this. "How many people were you taking in the evac?"

"Han, his wife and their granddaughter," Huang said. "The girl's mother and father were killed, and they're raising her."

"What was the plan?"

"We were supposed to get the three of them on a train to the coast," Huang said. "Had the tickets lined up and everything. Once there, we had a boat ready to take them to rendezvous with a navy ship in international waters."

"How old's the granddaughter?" Bolan asked.

"She's twelve," Yang said.

"What's the prison like?"

"Song Jing number ten," Herbie said. "Very big place. Many, many guards."

"How hard is it to get inside?" Bolan asked.

"No sweat," Herbie said. "My friend work in Song Jing. You pay money, I get you in."

"Getting in is not what I'm worried about," Bolan said. "It's getting out."

Herbie grinned again. "That take lots more money."

Bolan wasn't sure he could trust this guy, but at the moment he was stuck with him. He was stuck with all of them: two green agency kids—both fluent in Mandarin but short on experience—an incarcerated senior agent and a questionable Chinese collaborator. He couldn't wait until Grimaldi got there, but he could imagine Jack's reaction to all this.

"What kinds of weapons do you have?" Bolan asked.

Huang pulled back his jacket, exposing a Walther PPK .380.

"I've got one, too," Yang said.

"That's good." Bolan glanced at his watch. It was sixteen-twenty-five. They had a few more hours until Grimaldi's flight was scheduled to land. "Let's go check out the prison. I want to see what we're dealing with."

Huang and Yang exchanged glances. Bolan sensed they were holding something back. He stared at Huang. "What else do you want to tell me?"

Huang glanced at the young woman again, licked his lips, then said, "When Wayne and I were talking to Han, he refused to go with us. He insisted he has to stay in China until he gets some issues resolved. Han just wants us to take his family."

"He's not worried about his impending arrest?"

"I guess not." Huang shrugged. "He said he had some kind of insurance policy."

4

General Wong felt a trickle of sweat on his forehead and immediately wiped it off. Being summoned to Zhongnanhai, which housed the Politburo Standing Committee, the men who ruled China, meant that news of the American spy's capture and possibly the incident in Hong Kong had reached them. The massive walled compound made Wong nervous each time he entered. He knew it was a place where men, both soldiers and civilians, faced the ultimate tribunal. One word from the members of the Committee and he could be whisked away forever, without a trace. And depending on how much the Committee knew, it was possible that would be his fate today.

Wong was escorted down a long hallway by two armed guards, both of whom kept their faces expressionless. He longed to ask if they had any inkling of why he'd been summoned, but he knew better. Instead Wong thought about the captured spy and the stolen guidance system for the DF-21D anti-ship ballistic missiles—one of the closest-guarded secrets in China. If the Committee ever discovered that he'd agreed to sell even that early prototype version, they would place his head on a stake in the middle of Tiananmen Square. His act would be viewed as high treason. And to make matters worse, the prototype was now purportedly in the hands of the West.

So now Wong had to wonder how much this captured American was worth. Perhaps he could arrange a trade, the American for the prototype. But this would have to be done carefully to avoid discovery. Perhaps Chen could engineer it.

They came to a set of doors, and one of the guards pulled them open and stood at attention. The other entered and announced, "Esteemed ministers of the Standing Committee, General Wong Su Tong of the People's Liberation Army now stands before you, as ordered." The guard stepped aside and saluted as Wong marched forward.

The room itself was large enough to hold hundreds of standing spectators, but it was devoid of anyone except the seven men who sat behind the high, elongated bench. They were all smoking cigarettes and blowing the smoke upward toward the ridiculously high ceiling. Each of these men had his own secret agenda, which involved living in opulence while professing allegiance to the austere principles of the Party line. He knew they were secretly skimming money and padding their own clandestine bank accounts just as he, and virtually every other powerful government official, was doing. But he also knew that such corruption could exist only so long as it was not overtly displayed.

Or discovered.

Wong stepped up to the lectern in front of the bench and saluted. He removed his hat and placed it under his left arm, pressing it against his side. He hoped the perspiration hadn't yet begun to seep through the outer layers of his green uniform shirt.

"Members of the Standing Committee," Wong said

with a bow of respect. "I stand before you as your humble and obedient servant."

Zhu Song Lin, a small man with wire-rim glasses, spoke first. "General, it has come to our attention that you have arrested an American and are holding him in Song Jing Prison. Is this true?"

"It is, Minister Zhu."

"Is this American suspected of being a spy?"

Wong had to tread carefully here. He didn't know how much they already knew. If they caught him in a lie, his fate would be sealed.

"That matter is under investigation," Wong said, keeping his voice confident.

"And why was the Committee not immediately notified of this event?" Zhu asked.

Wong took a quick breath. "I was waiting to find out the entire story so I could present that to the Committee instead of unsubstantiated innuendos."

Silence, then Zhu whispered to Deng Ho Chin, the man sitting next to him. Deng was the senior member of the Committee and the one Wong knew he had to fear the most. Deng had lived through the Cultural Revolution in a "reeducation camp" in a remote province and had slowly risen back to power once Mao had died. Wong regarded him as the head of the serpent.

"So we do not know, as yet, the purpose of this American's presence?" Deng asked.

Again, Wong had to answer carefully. If he divulged too much, especially about the missing guidance system—which he believed the Committee didn't know about—he would open the door to his own arrest and interrogation. "He was speaking with a known dissident, but we have not yet determined the true nature of his presence here."

"And what are the Americans saying about this?"

"They have not been contacted as of yet," Wong said. "Nor have they inquired about the matter, to my knowledge."

"Your knowledge, it seems, is very limited," Deng said. He brought his cigarette to his lips. Wong held the man's stare as the ash glowed red. "Who is this dissident?"

"Han Son Chu," Wong said. "He is a lawyer representing a group of farmers in the Chung Ja Province in a land dispute. He is also well known to the—"

"We know who he is," Deng said. "And his popularity with the Western press. There is a movement underfoot by one of their celebrities to meet with Han, is there not?"

Wong nodded. "Yes, Minister."

Deng frowned. "And why is this Han not incarcerated? We do not need troublemakers running in the streets when the eyes of the world are upon us."

"He was placed under house detention," Wong said. "Pending the conclusion of the Games. It was thought more prudent to wait until they were completed and the Western news media had gone, to formally arrest and charge him."

"What is the basis of his grumbling?" another committee member asked. "Farmers and a land dispute?"

Wong's armpits felt sodden. His brother-in-law had bribed countless local officials to obtain the land necessary for his latest construction project. To reveal his own familial connection to the dispute could spell disaster. Wong would have to hope this connection had not come to the Standing Committee's attention.

"A local matter," Wong said. "Not worthy of notice by you and your esteemed colleagues."

Deng took another long drag on his cigarette and blew a plume of smoke from the corner of his mouth.

"Have the American brought here," he said. "Bring Han, as well. It is time to delve into this matter with more efficiency."

Wong felt a twinge in his bowels. Who knew what or how much Han had told the American? If he'd mentioned the dragon key and Wong's involvement with the Triad... If both of them were brought to Zhongnanhai Hall, they would be broken shortly thereafter. The interrogators here were the most ruthless in the world. Everything would be brought to light.

And a bright, harsh light will fall upon me, Wong thought. With the dragon key still not in his possession, fleeing to another country was not feasible. He would never survive, even if Chen agreed to hide him. Wong needed to stall for time until he found that damn dragon key. But how?

"It shall be done, Minister Deng," Wong said.

SONG JING PRISON was a twenty-minute drive away from the sprawl of the central part of the city. The identical high-rise apartment buildings seemed endless at first, but they finally gave way to stretches of older, more dilapidated houses. The prison itself sprang out of nowhere, an imposing, solid brick structure with massive concrete walls that were topped with concertina wire. There was barely any field space between the walls and the nearby residences. Guard posts adorned each corner and were also placed periodically along the top of the wall. Uniformed men with QBZ-95 rifles sat in each post. The tower at the front gate had a mounted machine gun on a turret.

The only bright spot was the main road to the

prison—where the clusters of buildings leading up to the front gate thinned a bit—but Bolan could see that between the gate and the first buildings was a long yard interspersed with walled sections. Two uniformed guards stood outside the barred gate smoking cigarettes, their rifles slung across their chests.

"The place looks like a fortress," he said as they drove past for the second time.

Herbie glanced in the mirrors nervously. "Hey, boss, maybe we better get outta here. We no want police seeing us drive by many, many times."

"Good idea," Bolan said. "You said you know somebody who works inside?"

"My friend," Herbie replied.

"What kind of job does he do in there?"

"He clean, sometimes cook."

A janitor who doubles as a cook, Bolan thought. Not exactly someone in authority, but on the other hand, someone invisible enough to have the run of the prison and overhear a lot of conversations.

"Can he get a message to Tressman?" Bolan asked.

Herbie shrugged. "He work now. I call later."

"He's got a cell phone?"

Herbie nodded and grinned. "He got number one cell phone. I got one, too."

"Then call him now," Bolan said. "Find out what kind of shape Tressman's in, exactly where in the prison he's at and anything else of importance."

"Okay, boss." Herbie took out his cell. "Right away."

"Monitor his conversation," Bolan said in a low voice to Huang.

Bolan glanced at his watch. Grimaldi's plane was due to land in a little over an hour. He told Herbie to head to the airport. The driver steered the van toward an expressway while cradling the cell phone on his shoulder, talking rapidly the whole time. When he hung up, Herbie shook his head. "Something up."

"Something's up about what?" Bolan asked. "Tressman?"

Herbie shook his head. "Don't know what, but he call me back. Maybe good news, maybe bad."

As soon as they were on an open stretch of road, Bolan took out his sat-phone and asked Herbie to pull over. Once the van stopped he got out and walked a few feet away to call Brognola. Huang got out of the van and walked in the opposite direction. Obviously it was time for him to check in, as well.

Brognola answered on the third ring.

"Any word on a diplomatic solution to our little problem?" Bolan asked.

"Not much," Brognola said. "The Chinese still haven't officially acknowledged that they've got him. They're stonewalling, waiting for us to make the first move."

"And?"

"And the President doesn't want to do that because it would be tantamount to admitting we had operatives working on the mainland during the big World Track and Field Games."

"Heaven forbid," Bolan said. He disliked politicians, diplomats and the games they played, especially when the stakes were high. To them it was like playing a game of chess, or in this case, mah-jongg, except a man's life hung in the balance. "Well, you might want to tell the President the place they're holding Tressman makes Fort Knox look like a Boy Scout camp."

Brognola sighed. "I was afraid of that."

"Can you email me some sat photos? If we're going to have to go in, I'll need as much info as I can get."

"Roger that, will do." Brognola cleared his throat. Bolan always took that to mean bad news was on the horizon. "I assume you tagged up with the newbies?"

"I did." Bolan glanced over at Huang, who was listening intently on his phone, his head bobbling up and down. "I'm with them now."

"Well, word is that Langley's in the process of sending them orders to abandon any side trips and continue at full speed with their original assignment. They're to let everything else get handled through diplomatic channels, and that includes Tressman."

"Diplomatic channels," Bolan said. He glanced at Huang, who now appeared more animated. "I really hate that phrase."

"Yeah," Brognola said. "Me, too, but what're you gonna do?"

"So they're supposed to let their team member dangle in the wind?" Bolan knew the President had a window of about twenty-four hours in which to request Tressman's release on the grounds of diplomatic immunity, but that was only after the Chinese acknowledged they had him. He wondered how long the poor guy could hold out without spilling everything. If his captors had indeed backed off on the beatings, as Herbie's inside man had said, maybe it was a sign that Tressman was already broken. "That's not the way I operate."

"I know." Brognola sighed again. "Look, I don't like it any more than you do. But that's Langley's decision, not ours. Did the newbies tell you what their assignment was?"

"Affirmative."

"Can you help them get back on track?"

"I could," Bolan said, "but first it would be nice to know what information's been compromised by that troubling little diplomatic matter."

Brognola chuckled. "That's what I figured you'd say. Look, I'm set to meet with the President this afternoon. I won't pull any punches. As soon as he's made a decision, I'll get back to you, okay?"

"Tell him not to take too long," Bolan said. "It's already tomorrow over here."

As SOON AS Wong was dismissed from the chamber, he jogged with careful deliberation to the nearby bathroom and vomited from both ends. He grabbed the stack of trimmed newspaper to clean himself, and pulled up his pants. Reaching into his pocket, Wong took out his cigarettes and lit one up as he flushed the mess away.

He needed to think. He needed help. There was only one person who could assist him now: that old bastard Chen.

Wong hated to become even more indebted to the Triad boss, but what choice did he have? He knew better than to call Chen while he was still inside Zhongnanhai. There were ears everywhere. He had no doubt one of the guards had been listening outside the bathroom door to the sounds of his purging.

Let the treacherous bastard bring that report back to Deng and the rest of them, Wong thought. Let it spoil the sumptuous dinner that was no doubt waiting for them.

As he stepped outside, he was surprised to see it was now dark. How long had he been in the hall? No matter. He walked briskly toward the gate that would let him out of this walled fortress. The driver and jeep that had delivered him here was still parked in the same spot by the curb. Wong strode to the vehicle and pulled open the door. The driver jerked to attention.

"Take me to my residence," Wong said. He needed to change clothes. And call Chen as soon as he could. Perhaps his sudden gastrointestinal attack was fortuitous after all. It gave him an excuse to delay dispatching the troops to pick up the American and Han.

As they drove through the crowded streets of downtown Beijing, they were slowed by the sea of cars. Wong struck his fist against the metal door and swore.

"Pull over there," he said. "I want to make a call."

The driver, who knew better than to question the general, grunted an affirmative response and stopped at the curb. Wong pulled open the door and got out. The stench inside the car was making him sick. He lit up another cigarette as he took out his cell phone and dialed. Chen didn't answer until the fifth ring.

"How are you, Comrade General?"

The bastard's voice sounded as calm as a lily floating in a pond.

"I have a new problem," Wong said. He quickly explained the orders given by the Committee and his concern about the consequences.

Chen remained silent for several seconds.

"Are you there?" Wong asked.

"I am."

"And did you not hear me? I don't know what to do. Do you have any ideas?"

"Most assuredly," Chen said. His voice sounded soothing, and Wong was surprised at the calming feeling it bestowed. "Here is what I need you to do."

5

Bolan was waiting just outside the customs checkpoint. After Grimaldi had his passport stamped and cleared the booth, he strode forward and greeted Bolan with a hearty handshake.

"Good to see you," he said.

"Likewise," Bolan replied.

As they headed for the exit, Bolan and Grimaldi talked about how excited they were to be covering the World Track and Field Games—just in case anyone was following them. They continued their innocuous conversation until they reached the van. Bolan chuckled as Grimaldi tossed his suitcase inside.

"Is that any way to treat a Louis Vuitton Pegase 65?" Bolan asked.

"That's my 45," Grimaldi said. "The 65's the bigger model. But I got a hunch that's going to be the least of my problems, right?"

Bolan made the introductions all around, noticing Grimaldi's less than enthusiastic handshakes with Yang and Huang. The Executioner knew he and Grimaldi shared a dislike of working with unknown Agency personnel in general, and newbies in particular. But in this case they had no options.

As they got into the van, Huang held up his smartphone. "I just got a text. Your package has arrived at the embassy."

"Ah." Grimaldi smiled. "It sounds like your baby and my SIG have arrived."

Bolan's "baby" was the Executioner's weapon of choice, a Beretta 93R. It was one of the few handheld pistols with a selector switch that allowed it to function in full-auto mode in three-round bursts.

"Let's set up a quick meet to get our equipment," Bolan said.

Huang nodded and sent a text back. The reply came about thirty seconds later with a location.

Herbie shifted into gear and they took off. Bolan kept watch out the rear window to check for anyone tailing them, but he saw no one.

"Were you able to get that helicopter lined up?" he asked Herbie.

The lopsided grin flashed in the rearview mirror. "No sweat, boss. Gotchu number one chopper, but I not fly."

"I've got somebody who can take care of that," Bolan said, grinning at Grimaldi.

"What? I just get off an eighteen-hour flight and I'm expected to jump right into a pilot's seat?" Grimaldi curled his head down and assumed a recumbent position. "Union rules. Wake me up in eight hours."

Yang and Huang looked at Grimaldi with widening eyes.

"He's a great kidder," Bolan said. "Besides being a fairly good pilot."

Grimaldi's head shot up. "What do you mean *fairly?*"

"I figured that would wake you up," Bolan said. "Herbie, what kind of helicopter did you get?"

"Number one chopper, boss."

"You get the exact kind I wanted?" Bolan looked at Yang, who said something in Mandarin.

Herbie listened, then began bobbling his head up and down. "Oh, okay. It China Tours helicopter. Very, very big, but no gun."

"No weapons," Yang added.

Bolan nodded. This was both good and bad, but hopefully, if they could smuggle Tressman out another way, they wouldn't have to land the chopper inside the prison. Not having any gun mounts would mean they'd be sitting ducks if things went south. Plus, he still didn't know how much he could trust Herbie. He talked a good game, and had delivered a few things thus far, but he was still a mercenary, and Bolan knew from experience that their loyalty was always available to the highest bidder. Still, the clock was ticking, and they had little choice if they wanted to get Tressman out.

"A China Tours helicopter," Grimaldi said. "What's the make?"

"Huh?" Herbie asked, his brow showing numerous wrinkles in the rearview mirror.

Yang started to translate, but Grimaldi waved dismissively. "Forget it. It isn't worth the time it'll take."

"But are you sure you can fly it?" Huang asked.

Grimaldi smirked. "Listen, pal, if it's got wings or rotors, I can fly it. Now, what's the plan?"

Bolan told Huang to call up the satellite pictures of the prison on his tablet. He then gave Grimaldi a quick update on the situation and the plan to rescue Tressman. Huang leaned over and held the screen so the other two men could see it.

"The place looks like a brick shithouse," Grimaldi said. "What kind of guns they got in those guard towers?"

"Looked like they had a big gun in that front tower," Bolan said.

"How big?"

"Maybe a fifty caliber."

"Aw, hell. And I thought this was gonna be hard." Grimaldi grinned. "Okay, do we have a contingency plan to deal with all these fortuitous circumstances?"

"Herbie's got a source inside the prison," Bolan said. "They've got shift change in four hours. His inside buddy said he can bring in extra workers tonight."

"Clean with honey-wagon," Herbie said.

"Honey what?" Grimaldi asked.

"It's a big vacuum truck that sucks out the sewage," Yang said. "Smells pretty awful."

"Ah," Grimaldi replied. "Something else to look forward to."

"Actually, that'll give us an advantage," Bolan said. "Nobody's going to want to check that truck too carefully. Herbie and Huang can go in, and the contact will lead them to Tressman. They remove him from his cell and smuggle him out in the truck. If that fails, plan B is for them to get up to the roof and call us." Bolan pointed to a flat section of roof on the satellite picture. "If we can sweep in and land here, it's at a higher elevation and far enough away from each of the guard towers that they won't have a clear shot. We pick them up and take off."

"That's a whole lotta ifs," Grimaldi said.

Bolan felt the same nagging doubts but had little choice. He didn't like sending Huang in with Herbie to tag up with the unknown inside man, but neither Bolan nor Grimaldi could pass for Chinese. At least Huang spoke the language. As a female, Yang would stand out way too much. Besides, Bolan had another assignment for her.

Grimaldi compressed his lips, obviously doing some mental calculations of his own. Finally he asked, "How much time we got before we have to start this misadventure?"

"About four hours." Bolan watched his reaction.

"All right," Grimaldi said. "Let me get this bird checked out. I want to make sure it's gassed up and ready to go."

"No ready now," Herbie said. "My friend say we must wait one hour." He held up his hand and rubbed his index finger and thumb together. "He want money up front. Twenty thousand yuan. We gotta pay for honey-wagon, too."

"Who's this guy again?" Grimaldi asked. "The piano player in the Geisha House?"

"Geisha?" Herbie asked.

"Jack." Bolan shot Grimaldi a knowing look, discouraging any more wisecracks, and said, "Right now he's the only game in town."

"Marvelous," Grimaldi said. "This just keeps getting better and better."

GENERAL WONG SIGNED the papers and put his official PLA seal next to his signature. Captain Xi stood at attention in front of the desk. Wong assessed the young officer. He was reasonably competent, had always performed well in the tasks he'd been assigned and was a graduate of the PLA Academy. Xi also had a reputation for strictly adhering to orders. Wong handed him the papers.

"You and three others will go to Song Jing Prison," Wong said. "At exactly twenty-one hundred, you will pick up a prisoner, remove him from the facility and contact me for further instructions. Me, personally. No one else. Do you understand?"

"Yes, Comrade General," the young officer said.

Wong gave him a long stare. The timing must be perfect.

"It is imperative that you do not arrive before twenty-one hundred," Wong said. "Is that clear?"

"Yes, Comrade General."

Wong felt the tug of a smile caress his lips. Xi's deference reminded Wong of himself in his younger days. He had no doubt that the instructions would be carried out to the letter. Perhaps Chen's plan would work after all. Perhaps…

"The prisoner you are to pick up," Wong said, thinking how to word his orders, "is not to be harmed, but he must be well secured at all times."

Wong waited for the inevitable "Yes, Comrade General."

"This prisoner is an American spy," Wong said. "It is not known if he speaks Mandarin, but we must operate on that assumption. He is not to be questioned during the transport. Do you have any questions as to your assignment?"

"No, Comrade General."

Wong took out a cigarette and lit it, letting Xi stand at attention throughout the entire ritual. He inhaled deeply and blew out a cloudy breath. "Once you have left the prison, a special contingent will escort you to Zhongnanhai. This transport is highly classified. It is particularly important that the foreign press, or any of their agents, is not alerted to the nature of this assignment. You and your men are sequestered to quarters until it is time for you to go. No communications with anyone. Is that understood?"

Xi's crisp reply pleased Wong. He dismissed the young officer and waited until the captain had softly closed the door to the office. Then Wong picked up his cell phone and called Chen.

"And have you forestalled the official arrest of Sammo Han and his family, as well?" The old bastard's voice sounded as soft as a woman's sometimes.

"Yes," Wong said. "That is set for tomorrow morning, after the American movie star attempts his meeting."

"Excellent. Everything is in place, as it should be. We have only to wait for the gentle rain to bring forth the blossoms."

Wong wasn't even bothered by the metaphor this time, but he knew he had a long way to go before his neck was out of the noose. He terminated the call and reviewed the plan for the next few hours. Captain Xi and his contingent would arrive at Song Jing, take custody of the American and then be met by Chen's men for an ostensible exchange. He pictured the process and felt a slight twinge of regret knowing he was sending Xi and the three other loyal soldiers of the People's Liberation Army to meet their death.

But they would die fulfilling their duty to their general. What more could a good soldier ask for?

BOLAN CHECKED THE spare magazines for his Beretta: one with armor-piercing rounds, three with standard loads and one jacketed with hollow points. He also had his five-and-a-half-inch folding Espada knife. In addition to Grimaldi's weapon of choice, a SIG Sauer P220, the package included night-vision goggles and bullet-proof vests for Bolan and Grimaldi, smoke and flash-bang grenades, thin leather gloves, special radios and more than enough yuan to pay any bills or bribes to get the job done.

The radios would be practically useless more than a few hundred feet apart due to the absence of any repeating towers tuned to their particular frequency. But it would still give Grimaldi and Bolan a communication advantage. He divided up the money, giving most of it to Grimaldi for storage, and kept a hefty roll for himself.

"Damn," Grimaldi said. "We could buy a couple dozen helicopters with all this."

"Hal must have figured we'd need some knocking-around money," Bolan said.

After paying off the attendant—who was supposed to be guarding the private airfield where the tourist agency kept its fleet of five helicopters—they'd flown the chopper, an old Russian Mi-8, to a small field about forty kilometers from the prison. Grimaldi wanted to do a more complete shake-down inspection after the cursory one he'd done at the airfield. The rendezvous point appeared to be a small, abandoned farm that was overgrown with weeds.

"If we're going to be banking our lives on this oil drum," Grimaldi said, "I want to go over it with a fine-tooth comb."

Bolan watched as his associate went over the helicopter, inspecting every inch with the scrutiny of a consummate professional. Grimaldi was perhaps the best pilot Bolan had ever known, and there was no one he'd rather have with him when his back was against the wall.

Bolan snapped the Beretta into his shoulder holster and slipped on a loose-fitting black BDU shirt. Underneath he wore a light Kevlar vest. It wouldn't stop high-velocity rounds from the guards' rifles, but he felt confident it would give him the edge against their standard Type 54 handguns. He fitted the Espada knife into the right-side pocket of his cargo pants and secured the extra magazines inside his jacket. He hoped this would go forward without a shot being fired. He wouldn't relish the consequences if it didn't. Taking on even a small contingent of the PLA on their home turf while being woefully underequipped would not be pleasant.

Bolan heard the whine of a truck's engine as a pungent odor wafted over the area. He turned and saw Herbie driving the honey-wagon. It was a medium-size truck with a big, oval-shaped tank on the back. Huang followed, driving Herbie's van. They doused their lights and pulled up into the field. There was very little cover since the entire area was devoid of trees.

"Heard from Yang?" Bolan asked Huang as the young man exited the van.

He nodded. "She's still at the market, waiting. Han's wife hasn't shown up yet."

Bolan had sent Yang to lay the groundwork for the evacuation of Han's wife and granddaughter the next morning. That operation was all set to unfold independently of tonight's. Splitting his meager force wasn't Bolan's first choice, but to proceed as Langley had directed—leaving Tressman to languish in a Chinese prison while the USA pursued his release through diplomatic means—wasn't an option. It would only be a matter of time before Tressman broke. For all Bolan knew, the beleaguered agent might have already broken, in which case, the official arrest of Han would probably be moved up. Some adjustments to the original evacuation plan were in order, too. It was best to operate on the assumption that the entire plan had been divulged.

"Hey," Grimaldi called. "How about some help over here? I need somebody to hold this light."

"I'll go," Huang said. "I always wanted to learn about helicopters."

Bolan nodded. At least the kid was game. Or maybe he just wanted to edge away from the smell of that honey-wagon. It didn't seem to bother Herbie, who grinned at Bolan and lit up a cigarette.

Bolan glanced at his watch: 2030. Almost time to move out.

He decided to check with Stony Man Farm one more time, just in case the powers in Washington had somehow managed a miracle for Tressman. He punched a number into the sat-phone, and when Brognola answered, Bolan asked, "Any progress?"

"Yeah, the boys here in D.C. have finally found someone as good at double-talk as they are. The Chinese are still stonewalling. Won't even admit they have him, much less talk about a diplomatic release or exchange. Not that we have any bargaining chips anyway."

"Well, in about an hour or so they might not, either."

Bolan could hear Brognola sigh. "I don't know if that's such a good idea, Striker. The odds seem a bit uneven."

"The odds stink," Bolan said. "We're also proceeding with instructions on the evac as far as we can."

"As far as you can? Problems?"

"Apparently one party is reluctant to dance," Bolan said, referring to Huang's report that Sammo Han wanted to remain in China. "Says he has unfinished business."

"Great," Brognola said.

"We're going to need a change in travel plans anyway. I'm not sure if the old file's been corrupted or not."

"Roger that. I'll get Aaron working on something right away. We'll set it up at this end and let you know."

Grimaldi waggled his flashlight up and down, signaling that he was ready to go. Bolan clicked his own light on and off in reply.

"Striker?" Brognola asked. "You there?"

"Yeah," Bolan said. "We're ready to shove off."

Brognola blew out a slow breath. "Is anything gonna go right on this damn mission?"

"I'll let you know soon enough," Bolan said as he terminated the call.

Bolan trotted over to the helicopter, glad to put as much distance between himself and the honey-wagon as possible. Herbie followed and the four men squatted as Grimaldi shone a flashlight over a map of the area and they went over the plan one more time.

"Herbie, is everything set?" Bolan asked.

"Everything number one," Herbie said, holding up his extended thumb.

"Your friend was able to give Tressman the instructions? He'll be ready?"

"Everything number one."

"Verify that before you go in," Bolan said.

Herbie looked slightly confused and Huang translated, after which Herbie nodded and took out his cell phone. Bolan looked at Huang. "You clear on your part?"

The kid nodded.

"Repeat it for me," Bolan said.

"Herbie's friend has the keys to the cell. We take Wayne out, and I stash him in the truck," Huang said. "Then the vacuum conveniently malfunctions and we have to leave."

"And if things go bad?" Bolan asked.

"I text you and we head for the roof. Wait for you to pick us up with the chopper."

Bolan hoped it wouldn't come to that. There were way too many variables for this to run smoothly.

"Remember to text me instead of calling," Bolan said. "I won't be able to hear the phone over the sound of those rotors. Plus, speaking English on a cell phone is a bit out of character for a guy driving a honey-wagon."

Huang grinned and nodded.

Bolan handed him a sealed plastic bag with a Glock 17 inside.

"You know where to put this," he said with a grin.

Huang smiled back and started heading for the vacuum hose attachment.

"Hey, boss," Herbie said. "How 'bout gun for me, too?"

Huang paused, but Bolan waved him on. "No gun. And you'll get your money once my people are safely out of Song Jing. Not before."

Herbie wrinkled his nose and nodded. "Okay, boss." He walked toward the truck.

Bolan and Grimaldi watched them take off as they synchronized their watches. It was 2043. Fifteen minutes to get to the prison, another twenty to twenty-five to get set up, get Tressman and do the pickup. Bolan and Grimaldi planned to be airborne and heading toward the rendezvous point at 2120. They didn't have the fuel to be in the air the entire time, plus a tourism chopper circling in the nighttime skies over this section of the city was bound to attract undue attention. Bolan mulled it all over and blew out a slow breath.

Way too many intangibles, he thought.

The taillights of the honey-wagon were two minute red dots now.

Bolan's phone vibrated with an incoming text. It was from Yang.

Meeting complete. Set for tomorrow.

Bolan acknowledged the message, told her to stay put and gave Grimaldi an update.

"This whole thing stinks almost as bad as that honeywagon," Grimaldi said, nodding toward the truck. "You think the kid can handle it?"

Bolan didn't answer. He'd been wondering the same thing. They waited for twenty minutes, going through their equipment one more time, and finally started the preflight checklist. Herbie and Huang should have gotten inside the prison by now. It was time to get airborne. As they were working, Bolan's cell phone vibrated with an incoming text. He glanced at the screen and his heart sank.

This one was from Huang: Problem.

10-4, Bolan texted back. Sitrep.

"Something's up," Bolan said.

Grimaldi's head shot up. "What?"

Bolan held up his phone. "Waiting for more info."

"Marvelous," Grimaldi said.

Five minutes, seeming like five hours, slowly passed, then another text came from Huang: PLA picking up T now. Departure imminent.

The Chinese army was taking Tressman out of the prison? Bolan assessed this new complication. They were obviously taking him to a new location, but why? Had their rescue op been compromised? He wished he could talk to Huang directly, but didn't want to risk it.

Roger that, Bolan texted back. How many? What vehicle, ETD?

4 PLA, Huang replied. Red army deuce-and-a-half. ETD in 5 to 10.

This isn't making sense, Bolan thought. Why would they send a four-person transport squad in a two-and-a-half-ton truck?

Regardless, Bolan knew they had to get airborne and track the departure. At least a vehicle that size would be easy to spot. If the opportunity for an interdiction arose, they'd take it, and if not, it was back to square one. He slipped on his night-vision goggles and gave Grimaldi a sitrep.

We'll tag them, Bolan texted to Huang. Break down and get out ASAP.

He slipped the satellite phone into his pocket and put on the helicopter headphones so he and Grimaldi could communicate. The engine rumbled and then cycled to life as the big rotors began their incremental acceleration.

"You read me?" Grimaldi asked via the headphones.

"Loud and clear."

Grimaldi flipped one goggle down over his left eye but kept the right one up to maintain his depth perception during liftoff.

"I gotta tell you," he said, "I got a bad feeling about this one."

"You and me both," Bolan replied.

They ascended into the black sky. The lights of the city glowed far to the east. Below them the ground looked dark and unforgiving. Grimaldi leveled off at about one thousand feet and headed for the prison. When they got within a few kilometers he pushed the stick forward and they descended to five hundred.

"Keep your eyes open for any power lines," he said, flipping the other goggle down into place.

Bolan used a pair of night-vision binoculars to search the maze of buildings below, and finally found the front gate of the prison. He suddenly wondered if the PLA truck would be leaving by that exit. Grimaldi continued in a slow circle.

"I sure hope they don't hear us and decide to open up with that fifty cal," he said.

"You and me both," Bolan replied, but he doubted the guards would be that reckless. A helicopter flying in the vicinity at night would most likely be taken for a military or police aircraft.

At the very least, he told himself, they'll think it's a news station.

The front gates opened and a huge truck exited the prison.

"That has to be them," Bolan said.

"A Chinese army deuce-and-a-half? How many bogies we dealing with?"

"Huang says four."

"Four?" Grimaldi laughed. "How big are they?"

"They might be giants," Bolan said. He continued to track the vehicle as it wound through the narrow streets.

"That reminds me of an old George C. Scott movie," Grimaldi said. "He played this mental patient who thought he was Sherlock Holmes."

"We might need old Sherlock to figure out what's going on here."

They ascended a few hundred feet, allowing them to follow the truck without the sound of the rotors announcing their presence. To Bolan's surprise, the vehicle turned away from the road leading back to the center of the city and continued to an open field. He adjusted the binoculars and saw the dark shape of an automobile, a van, parked off the roadway.

"Looks like they're tagging up with somebody," he said.

Grimaldi canted the helicopter to give him a better vantage point. "Want me to go lower?"

"We're good." Bolan could see a group of people getting out of the van.

"I wish we had an infrared scanner on this thing," Grimaldi said. "It isn't *Dragonslayer,* that's for sure."

"I'm counting eight exiting the van below," Bolan said. The figures assembled along the road and waited as the army truck rolled up to their position. The driver and the passenger got out of the big truck, walked to the group on the roadway. After a few more seconds Bolan saw three figures getting out of the back of the deuce-and-a-half. One of them moved with extreme slowness and needed assistance.

It had to be Tressman.

Suddenly the figures below whirled in a dance of confusion. Several pinpoint flashes sparkled in the darkness. Two figures fell by the front of the truck. The three at the rear were motionless as the others surrounded them. They took one of them to the van and walked the other two to the side of the road, where they were made to kneel.

Two more starbursts of light flashed in the inky blackness, and the two kneeling figures toppled over.

Two of the eight people from the van began picking up the fallen bodies and tossing them into the back of the army truck. Then they all got into the van, which started up and did a three-point turn on the roadway.

"Which one?" Grimaldi asked. "The new van or the old deuce-and-a-half?"

"Stay with the van," Bolan said. They were too far to know for certain, but Bolan was willing to bet that Tressman was now in custody of whoever was driving it. They'd just executed four PLA soldiers without the slightest compunction, which meant they were not only brutal, but also probably operating outside the law.

Triad involvement? That seemed likely. But why had the soldiers stopped to meet them? It had all the earmarks of an arranged rendezvous, except for the surprise ending. Soldiers operated on orders, as did the Triad, but each reported to an entirely different set of bosses.

All that could be sorted out later. Right now Bolan had one shot at getting Tressman back, and that was to grab him before he disappeared into the morass of the Triad's network. But with Yang, Huang and Herbie out of the picture, and Grimaldi piloting the helicopter, the Executioner had little choice but to do this next part alone.

6

The Mantis braced himself against the van's rear fender and watched as the doctor and his female attendant administered to the American spy. The ham-handed interrogators inside Song Jing had beaten him to a pulp. The man's eyes were swollen shut and his face was distorted with so many bruises that his features were almost unrecognizable. The Mantis was amazed the American had not yet been broken. The man was apparently stronger than he looked.

"What is his condition?" the Mantis asked.

He'd been told the American was fluent in Mandarin, so he operated under the assumption that the spy was listening and understanding the conversation.

"He's been severely beaten," the doctor said. "But he should recover, with rest."

The Mantis nodded and said, this time in English, "Proceed as directed."

The doctor reached into his medical bag and withdrew a hypodermic syringe and a small vial of clear liquid. He glanced down at the American, apparently estimating the man's weight, and then stuck the end of the needle into the soft rubber stopper and nodded. The nurse tied a soft rubber hose around the American's left biceps, then began massaging the inner aspect of his elbow. The Mantis moved forward, kneeling next to the American.

"Can you hear me, brother?" he asked softly in English. It was important for the American to think he'd been rescued by friends.

The five Triad henchmen wouldn't understand the conversation, and it didn't matter if the doctor and nurse did. The Mantis had worked with them on numerous occasions on everything from treating wounded gangsters to adversarial interrogations, which this was. Expediency was the primary goal here, and hence, deception was the necessary medium along with the drug. If the American had not broken under the brutal beating, a more subtle approach was called for.

The Mantis leaned closer to the American, placing his lips next to the man's ear.

"Can you hear me?" he asked in a soft whisper. "We're going to help you. Are you in pain?"

The American said nothing.

The Mantis motioned for the doctor to administer the sodium pentothal. He leaned forward, pausing to adjust to the motion of the van over the roadway, and sank the end of the needle into the distended vein on the American's arm.

"Listen, brother," the Mantis said in English. "We're giving you a shot to relieve the pain. We have taken you from the prison and we're on our way to a safe house and then the American embassy. Do you understand?"

The American still said nothing, and the Mantis wondered if the man's jaw might be broken. Still, he wasn't ready to give up and wanted to get the man talking.

"Does Sammo Han know you were taken?" he asked. He knew the Americans would be referring to Han Son Chu by his English name.

"Sammo Han," the American repeated.

"Right," the Mantis said. "Do we need to contact him about the plan?"

"The plan…"

"The escape plan," the Mantis whispered. "Has it been compromised? We need to move soon."

"New plan," the American said. His voice sounded a bit stronger now.

The Mantis looked at the doctor, who smiled and nodded.

"We want to proceed with the new plan," the Mantis said. "What is it?"

"Be at the central station at noon," the American said. "Call Jimmy Tai Pang for the tickets." He rolled off a set of digits that the Mantis took to be a phone number. His words had a rote sound to them, as if he'd committed the information to memory long ago and was now dragging it up to the surface. The drug had obviously lulled him into a state of compliance. "Call Jimmy Tai Pang for the tickets," he repeated.

The Mantis took a chance. He didn't know how much longer the American's garrulousness—and consciousness, for that matter—would last.

"Right, I remember. Give me his cell phone number again," he said, motioning for the nurse to give him a pen and paper. She handed him her mini notebook just as the American mumbled off the numbers.

The Mantis scribbled them down and told him to repeat them one more time. This repetition matched the first. He tried to think what else he would need.

The curtain separating the front of the van from the rear section tore open, and one of the idiots poked his head through.

"Boss, there's a helicopter close by."

The Mantis looked up angrily. The guy's head disappeared in a flash and the curtain was pulled back into place.

"Helicopter?" the American said. "PLA military or US?"

US? Did this fool actually think the Americans could manage a rescue inside mainland China? The Mantis smiled at the absurdity and leaned close, keeping his voice soothing and calm.

"That's right," he whispered. "It's one of ours. It'll take you to the American embassy soon. Now, what is Jimmy Tai Pang going to do for us?"

"He's got the tickets."

"Tickets? What tickets?"

"For the train. Sammo's wife…granddaughter…three of us… Reservations."

"Reservations to where?"

"Qingdao."

So the plan was to escape Beijing by train with Han and his family.

"Jimmy Tai Pang," the Mantis said. "Do the others on your team know him by sight?"

"No. Never saw him. Just dealt…with…me." The American coughed, his breathing turning sonorous, as though he was tiptoeing on the edge of a deeply induced slumber.

The Mantis asked one more question. "What about the dragon key?"

"Key? What key?"

"The flash drive," the Mantis whispered. "From the general."

"Huh?" The American licked his swollen and discolored lips. His voice sounded cracked when he answered. "Don't know…"

"Where? Where is it hidden?"

"Hid...? What?" His breathing slowed, thickened, catching in his throat.

The Mantis shook him. "Where is it hidden?"

"Don't know," the American said. "Only he... Don't... Must go to...Shanghai." The man drifted into silence. The Mantis slapped his cheeks, trying to rouse him to no avail.

"He's totally under the anesthetic now," the doctor said.

The Mantis nodded. He had enough information for the time being, and some leads to follow. He reached up and pulled the curtain back, glaring at the front-seat passenger who had dared to interrupt him.

"How much longer till we arrive at the house?" the Mantis asked.

"We're almost there," the man said. "Perhaps ten minutes."

The Mantis pulled the curtain back in place.

He would have to call Master Chen soon and advise him of these developments.

FROM THEIR AERIAL perch, Bolan and Grimaldi watched the van's progress as they headed toward the outskirts of the city. This was no major urban area, but rather clusters of smaller, older houses that were probably on the chopping block of some urban renewal program. The groups of boxlike structures were separated by tiny walkways and encompassing walls. It looked a few steps above a shantytown.

If the van got too deep into the massive Beijing infrastructure, following them by air would be next to impossible. So would a vehicular tail, even if Huang and Herbie could manage to catch up. Bolan texted Huang again asking for a sitrep, but figured a reply would come later rather than sooner. Huang and Herbie still had to extricate themselves from the prison and ditch the honey-wagon for their other vehicle. The honey-wagon might make a tail less conspicuous, but the bad guys would certainly smell them coming.

Bolan began searching the cabin for whatever equipment he could find. Best-case scenario, the bad guys would take Tressman to an isolated location that would be immediately accessible. Worst case, Grimaldi would have to set up an ambush by landing the chopper in anticipation of the van's route. Bolan knew there wasn't much chance of winning a firefight against the six killers he'd seen execute the PLA soldiers. Plus, with Tressman in the vehicle, he would inevitably be in the field of fire. If his captors didn't kill him immediately, one of Bolan's bullets might do the job for them.

No time to play the what-if game, he thought. The glove box by the copilot's seat contained a logbook, a pen and some paper with Chinese characters scribbled on it. Clipped underneath the console he found a box containing a flare gun and three flares. After removing the box, he told Grimaldi he was going to look farther in the cabin.

"Let me know if you find any fortune cookies," Grimaldi said. "We need a couple of good ones."

Bolan grinned in spite of the dour mood. He slipped off his earphones, unbuckled his seat belt and squeezed between the seats.

The rear cabin was spacious. It could hold at least twenty-five to thirty passengers. It was also fairly Spartan. Not much in the way of extra materials. He did find a substantial coil of nylon rope, however. There were also a set of D-rings fastened to a metal loop on the side of the cabin. The rope seemed close to three hundred feet. Certainly long enough for a quick rappel to the ground.

Bolan unclipped his Espada knife, pulled the closest seat belt to its full extension and then sliced the flat material off close to the base. Repeating this with the next seat belt, he finally had enough for a makeshift Swiss seat. He tied the knots as tightly as he could, then tugged on them. Satisfied it would support his weight, he worked the D-ring over the top strand and tested the flexibility of the nylon rope going through it.

It should get me to the ground, he thought. Bolan went forward and put the headset back on.

"I've got enough stuff to do about a three-hundred-foot rappel," he said.

Grimaldi grinned. "Give or take a few feet, I imagine?"

Bolan laughed. There would be no way to determine exactness in this drop. But desperate times, as the saying went…

"And that half-ass Swiss seat," Grimaldi added. "It looks like something the ragman dragged out of a Dumpster."

"I'm sorry I'm not measuring up to your high sartorial standards." Bolan's cell phone vibrated with an incoming text. Huang had responded to the sitrep query.

Leaving Song Jing now. Where you at? Before Bolan could reply, Grimaldi pointed downward. "The van's slowing down."

Bolan used his night-vision binoculars to track the vehicle. The brake lights flashed suddenly and the van turned left onto a narrow roadway. It kept going until it got to an enormous cluster of little single-story houses, all of which sat back-to-back, separated by a series of high walls. From above, it looked like a maze. Each house was shaped like an L and opened into a tiny courtyard.

"Looks like a regular gated community, don't it?" Grimaldi said. "Sort of like a Chinese version of Brentwood."

"Complete with outdoor plumbing."

Bolan refocused the binoculars and watched the van turn left onto a smaller, narrower roadway that led into the maze of houses. It pulled down to an intersecting street and stopped next to a field of broken bricks and piles of trash. The doors of the van opened and a group of eight people got out. Two of them carried a limp form. They moved about thirty meters toward the group of houses on the left. The houses were separated by walkways that appeared to provide only three feet of space between each of the structures.

The men opened a gate and carried the unconscious man inside, going into the house on the right side of the courtyard.

Bolan turned to Grimaldi. "I've got to get down there. Think you can pick us up once I get Tressman?"

Grimaldi scanned the area and shook his head. "Looks like some power lines over the houses. I could try to set it down on the main road, but there's more lines going off that way." He snorted. "That vacant lot where the van parked looks like our best bet. It'll still be like trying to parallel park a school bus in a slot designed for a Volkswagen, but it's about all that's open."

"Guess I'll get a chance to test this out," Bolan said, tugging on his makeshift harness one more time as he picked up the coil of rope. "Drop me on top of that house across the street from where they went in."

Bolan went to the door, pulled it open and felt the

rush of the cool night air. The syncopated whirling of the rotor blades drowned out every other sound. He searched for somewhere to tie off that would hold his weight. Bolan finally decided on the metal rung that held the passenger seat in place. He would lose about two or three feet of rope doing the tie-off, but it was the closest thing he could find to a cleat.

He dropped the rope out the door and watched it uncoiling like a snake spiraling through the darkness. As far as he could tell, it stopped a bit short of the roof.

"Bring her down about twenty feet," Bolan said.

"Roger that."

As the helicopter descended a bit more, Grimaldi said, "Just so you know, we're getting low on gas. You'll have to make this quick unless you want to walk back to our original rendezvous point."

Bolan nodded. Once he took off the headset he and Grimaldi would be incommunicado. He couldn't expect Grimaldi to keep hanging around until he ran out of gas or tangled with some Chinese Mi-17s armed with miniguns.

"Okay," Bolan said. "Give me five minutes, ten max. If you don't see my signal, go back to the field area and meet Huang. Text him to meet us there in your spare time."

"What spare time?" Grimaldi asked. "Flying this bucket of bolts is a two-handed, full-time job."

Bolan smiled. "I'll rappel down, get Tressman and go to the LZ. I'll fire a flare when I'm ready." He looked down through the green-tinged viewfinder. It was time to move. He slipped on his thin leather gloves and started to remove the headset when Grimaldi's voice stopped him.

"Watch your six," he said.

Bolan nodded. "Watch for my flare. See you in five, hopefully." And with that, he slipped off the headset and stepped to the edge of the open doorway.

The Executioner tested the knots of the rope and moved out on the right-hand landing skid. Leaning backward, he went to an almost horizontal position to assure he wouldn't flip back and strike his head on the thick metal skid as he shoved off. In the next moment he was zipping downward in the darkness, feeling the nylon cord slip through his fingers as it ran through the D-ring. He paused after he'd gone about two hundred feet and glanced down. The rope whirled and twisted below him due to the wash from the rotors. Bolan dropped about fifty feet more.

Still difficult to judge if he had enough rope.

Twenty feet…

Twenty more, and stop.

He held the nylon cord between his thumb and forefinger, against the middle of his back, and rechecked the distance one more time. The rope was a bit short of the roof. How much, he couldn't really tell. His depth perception was thrown off by the night-vision goggles and his awkward, hovering position. Finding a frame of reference was next to impossible. But the clock was ticking and he had little choice but to keep going.

Bolan released his grip on the line and dropped downward again, suddenly feeling the last of the rope snake through the gloved fingers of his right hand, his brake hand. The rope whipped around his right side and out through the D-ring. He tried to grab hold of the evasive line with his left but felt it slip through his grasp as he went into total free fall.

A second later his body collided with the tiled roof and the Executioner felt the wind knocked out of him.

The fall had been about fifteen feet, and he was already starting a fast roll down the sloping roof. He reached out, trying to grab something to stop his movement. His chest ached as he struggled to breathe.

Bolan continued to slide. Turning on his side, he extended his left hand and reached for the Espada knife with his right. The dark edge of the roof seemed only a few feet away, and he wondered about the distance of the next drop. And what he'd be landing on. Suddenly his left side struck something hard.

A small, round chimney.

Bolan managed to curl his body around it, sucking in a few shallow breaths.

Voices came from below, inside the house. It was time to move. He extended his body downward, hooking the instep of his left boot around the chimney and lowering his head to the edge of the roof. The drop to the ground looked to be about twelve to fifteen feet.

Easy enough, he thought, and slipped his left foot loose. Bolan swiveled as he slid downward, gliding over the ripple of tiles. A split second later he landed on his feet on solid ground. Solid concrete to be more exact. He heard more voices shouting inside the house. Bolan ran down a narrow walkway, suddenly feeling something scurrying around his feet.

Rats. Lots of them.

He noticed something else, too. A pungent odor reminiscent of the honey-wagon. About eight feet in front of him he saw a small outhouse. He continued running and reached for the roof, pulling himself up and over the structure. Bolan dropped onto a narrow pathway that ran between the houses on the other side. More rats scurried around his boots. On the other side of the wall he could hear more yelling, accompanied by the shrill cries of rodents.

And I thought I'd have to do this alone. He smiled and pulled the Beretta 93R from his shoulder holster. After attaching the sound suppressor, he moved toward the main walkway.

The Executioner paused at the juncture of the small alleyway and what might be considered the intersecting street. It was only about fifteen feet wide and composed of uneven cobblestones. He estimated that the target house was two doors down, across the street. At the moment, the street seemed relatively deserted. Two men walked perhaps fifty feet down the block.

Not the optimal time or conditions for moving, but the clock was ticking.

Bolan jammed the Beretta back into the holster, crossed the narrow expanse in three quick steps and pushed through the wooden gate in front of the house directly across from him. At this point hesitation would be suspicious. Bolan stepped inside a small courtyard.

A large metal tub of water sat next to a pipe and faucet to his left. Two women, who were cooking with a small portable stove set into one of the walls, looked up in surprise. Bolan nodded to them and crossed the small courtyard in two steps, heading for the wall that separated this house from the target one. It appeared to be about seven feet high. As he reached up to grab the top of the wall he got a quick look at dozens of pieces of broken glass imbedded in the concrete. He was wearing gloves but didn't want to risk a cut on the jagged shards. He looked around and spied a large rug hanging up nearby. The Executioner grabbed it and thrust it over the top of the wall as the two women yelled at him in shrill displeasure.

Ignoring them, he vaulted over the wall, landing in an almost identical courtyard on the other side. This one was deserted, however.

The Executioner headed down a small aisle to the back of the property, noting the powerful odor of human waste. He heard grunting and scraping sounds behind him, and the door to the outhouse burst open. A squatting man peered out, his pants around his shins, brandishing a Norinco Type 54 semiauto in his right hand. Bolan shot him in the forehead. The man fell over, exposing a dark hole in the concrete floor. Leaving him where he was, Bolan moved to the corner and took a quick look.

The construction was the same as the other houses: L shaped with a small courtyard. A three-foot pipe with a spigot rose from the concrete and spewed a stream of water into a metal tub that sat next to the solid wooden gate. The hooch had a sliding door, but Bolan could see lights on behind it. He heard voices, too. The door opened and a man appeared, shouting something in Mandarin. Another Norinco pistol hung loosely in the man's grip.

Eight hostiles had moved from the van with the unconscious man. Bolan had to assume all of them were armed, and certainly dangerous. He also didn't know if there were additional personnel in the house prior to their arrival. Facing those kinds of odds meant his only chance was the element of surprise. He pulled a flashbang grenade from the pocket of his cargo pants and straightened the flanges of the pin.

The guy in the doorway laughed and yelled again.

Probably wants to know what's taking his buddy so long in the latrine, Bolan thought.

He switched the Beretta to his left hand and pulled

the pin on the flash-bang. The Executioner was adept at shooting with his nondominant hand, but successfully throwing the grenade through the slight opening between the door and the jamb required the accuracy of his right hand.

The guy in the doorway yelled again, louder this time, and opened the door a bit wider as he stepped down into the courtyard, his face twisting into an angry scowl.

Bolan extended his left arm around the corner, acquired a sight-picture, and fired in one smooth motion. The man twisted and fell on the ground. Another man peered out and looked down at his fallen comrade. Bolan shot him in the side of the head and stepped into the courtyard, releasing the safety flange on the flash-bang. He threw it through the open space with an easy underhand toss, switched the Beretta back to his right hand and waited for three more seconds until the concussive blast of the grenade burst through the open space.

Moving forward, Bolan kicked the sliding door back on its slot and extended his right arm, with the Beretta, inside the room. Wisps of smoke and a distinct smell of burned gunpowder hung in the air. At the far end, a man and a woman were kneeling beside a supine figure Bolan took to be Tressman, a medical bag next to them. The other two occupants of the room were standing, shaking their heads. These two both had submachine guns slung in front of their hips. Bolan shot them Mozambique-style, two in the chest, one in the head. He then stepped inside the room and slammed the door.

The man and woman were hunched over Tressman now, blinking their eyes with expressions of disorientation and discomfort. Bolan kicked the man in the side, sending him sprawling. He was a bit more gentle with the woman, grabbing her by the arm and lifting her up. He did a quick, but thorough, frisk. Finding nothing, he shoved her down into the corner and frisked the man. He was unarmed, as well.

Bolan shoved him next to the woman and said, in one of the few Mandarin commands he knew, "Don't move."

Bolan went to one knee, keeping the Beretta trained on the two of them, and checked Tressman's carotid for a pulse. The beat was slow and steady. Bolan managed to peel open Tressman's distended left eyelid and saw a glazed whiteness. The medical bag was open, and a hypodermic syringe, a rubber tourniquet and a vial lay on top of what appeared to be a stethoscope and a blood pressure cuff. The vial contained some type of clear liquid.

Bolan stood and moved over to the man and the woman. They were gradually coming around. Stepping over an expanding puddle of blood from one of the corpses, he spotted a large ball of heavy twine in one corner and holstered the Beretta. Using the twine, he secured the woman's hands behind her back and then bound her knees and ankles. Satisfied that she was immobile, Bolan moved to the man. He was almost completely recovered from the debilitating effects of the blast by the time Bolan had finished securing his wrists, knees and ankles. As Bolan stood, he saw the man's brown eyes open wide behind a pair of metal-rimmed glasses. The man assessed the Executioner carefully, then said, "You are an American."

Bolan didn't answer.

"Please," he said. "Do not kill us. We are not Triad. We are medical professionals."

The guy's English was good, and he didn't have the

look of a gangster. Even though the clock was ticking, Bolan decided to see what he could find out.

"Where's the other guy?"

The man's brow crinkled. "I don't understand."

"I saw nine people enter this room." Bolan made an all-encompassing gesture. "I've accounted for eight. Where did the last one go?"

"He left soon after we arrived. I do not know where."

"Who was behind this?" Bolan asked.

The man shook his head. "I cannot tell you that. They will kill me."

Bolan's lips stretched into what he hoped would be a malevolent grin. "And I'll kill you if you don't." He let the grin fade away and set his features into a scowl. "You got three seconds to tell me."

The man fidgeted.

Bolan pulled open his shirt and put his hand on the butt of the Beretta. The man's eyes widened.

"All right," he said. "It was Lee Son Shin. They call him the Praying Mantis."

Bolan had heard about a legendary Triad enforcer who went by that name, but other than a few reports citing crimes allegedly committed by the Mantis, Bolan knew little else. He glanced at his watch. He'd been at this game for almost eight minutes. It was time to get moving. He gestured at Tressman.

"How bad is he?"

"Very bad. He needs medical attention. I can give it to him. Please, let me live. I am a doctor."

"A doctor who works for the Triads," Bolan said. He picked up the vial. "What's this?"

The doctor's eyes flashed to the left. "Penicillin."

"Try again," Bolan said.

The doctor swallowed quickly. "It's sodium pentothal. But they made me administer it. I had no choice."

"I'll bet," Bolan said. He dumped the contents of the medical bag onto the floor but saw no other medications. He picked up two rolls of gauze and one of medical tape. The woman had come out of her stupor and was lying on her side, crying.

"How much of the drug did you give him?" Bolan asked.

The doctor blinked and shook his head. "Only a few cubic milliliters. It will not harm him. He needs to sleep anyway."

Bolan pulled out his knife. "How long will he be out?"

The doctor's eyes widened, a look of terror on his face. "What are you going to do with that?"

"How long?"

"A few hours perhaps," the doctor said. "Please, I've cooperated. You must let me go."

Bolan sliced off some material from a shirt hanging nearby. He went to the woman first, telling her to open her mouth and then tying a gag in place.

"You cannot leave us here," the doctor said. "They'll kill us."

"I doubt that. Good doctors are probably hard to come by in China. Especially Triad doctors."

"No, no," the doctor said, shaking his head furiously. "You do not understand. This area is not safe for us. The people around here are disenfranchised peasants. They have a hatred for those in the medical profession. If they find us, they might kill us. It's quite common here."

"Then you'd better hope your buddy the Mantis finds you first." He secured the gag. It would have been quicker and safer to kill both of them, but the Executioner didn't kill unless it was necessary, and these two were basically civilians. He rechecked the bonds then stood up and moved over to Tressman.

It was time to go.

Bolan squatted down and lifted Tressman, slinging the unconscious man over his left shoulder like a sack of potatoes. Tressman was probably about a hundred and eighty pounds of pure dead weight at this point, but that barely slowed Bolan down. He stepped out into the small courtyard and moved to the gate. After checking to make sure the alleyway was clear, Bolan stepped through the gate, closing it behind him, and began a quick trot toward the vacant lot about thirty yards away. As he ran, his fingers closed over the handle of the flare gun in his right pocket. Withdrawing the gun, Bolan cocked back the hammer, pointed it upward and pulled the trigger.

The crisp pop and the accompanying trail of bright light and smoke sailed upward through the nighttime sky. Before he'd gone fifty feet Bolan heard the staccato beating of the approaching rotors. Grimaldi was right on time.

7

General Wong was nervous, but he knew better than to express this to Chen. The Triad leader was his only chance to keep this situation contained. And the old bastard knew it.

The son of a whore has me by the testicles, Wong thought. He adjusted his pants at the unpleasant thought and picked up the cell phone, scrolling down to Chen's private number.

Last night Wong had been informed about the "abduction" of the American spy, and he needed to make the proper notifications to the Politburo this morning. The Standing Committee would be summoning him soon, and when they did, he'd be able to tell them that he'd recovered the American, and the foreign agents who'd taken him, by killing the contingent of soldiers. It would be unfortunate that all of the foreigners had perished during the recovery operation. You couldn't interrogate dead men.

Hopefully, Chen's assassin had obtained whatever information they needed from the American, Tressman.

Regardless, it was time to see how things were progressing. He pressed the button for Chen's number.

It rang several times, and Wong glanced at his watch.

It was 0500. Early, but still reasonable enough to give him time to prepare.

Finally, Chen's voice came on the phone, sounding as fresh as someone who was wide-awake. Wong had no time for formalities. "I've been waiting for your call. Did your men get the American?"

"They did."

Wong felt a wave of relief. "What have you found out?"

Silence.

"Are you there?" Wong asked.

"There has been a slight complication," Chen said. He paused, as if enjoying the silence and the anxiety he knew it must be causing Wong.

"Complication?"

"After we seized him, several of my men were killed by an American agent who took the prisoner."

"What?" Wong was flabbergasted. "How could the Americans manage that?"

"Apparently they are more resourceful than we anticipated," Chen said. "But do not be concerned. A wise man plans for every convolution."

"What does that mean?"

"I have the situation well in hand," Chen said.

"Well in hand?"

"Of course, Comrade General."

Wong hated it when Chen called him that. There was condescension lurking behind his obsequiousness. The Triad leader's soft chuckle came over the phone's speaker like the ticking of a clock—a clock connected to a detonator.

"And what am I supposed to tell the Committee when they summon me this morning?" Wong asked.

"Tell them your men were assassinated by some mercenaries believed to be employed by the Americans," Chen said. "The spy was already interrogated and is of little importance now. There is something else you must do. Something more pressing."

Wong bit his lower lip as he pulled a cigarette out of his pack and lit it. "What is that?"

"Are your men standing by to arrest Han Son Chu this morning?"

"Yes," Wong said. "The Committee directed it, but they are to wait until after the American movie star leaves."

He heard Chen's soft chuckle once again. "Excellent. Here is what you must ensure happens."

BOLAN GLANCED AT his watch and told Herbie to drive around the block again. He'd slept about three hours in the past forty-eight and he could feel felt a wave of fatigue beginning to wash over him.

What I wouldn't give for a cup of coffee, he thought. Even some of Aaron's horrible brew.

"At least they drive on the right side of the road here on the mainland," Grimaldi said. "Not like in Hong Kong."

He sounded as tired as Bolan. The three men continued to circle the streets near the bus station, waiting for Yang.

Early that morning, Bolan had met Han's wife and granddaughter at the marketplace and whisked them away after telling them the evac plan had changed. Instead of heading to the coast by train, Bolan would put them on a bus with Huang.

When Tressman had come to, he'd admitted he wasn't sure how much of the previous plan he'd divulged under the interrogations.

"I feel like I let everybody down," he'd said. "I let the Agency down, too."

Bolan hadn't had the heart to tell him the Agency was letting him dangle in the wind. At this point the injured man needed something to hold on to. "You did fine, under the circumstances," Bolan said. "Now help us get the rest of the mission completed."

Tressman had nodded and Bolan had wrapped the man's face with gauze and taped it in place. Then Tressman, Mrs. Han and the granddaughter had headed for the bus station, with Huang riding shotgun. They'd been hoping to pass for a Chinese family transporting an injured uncle down to the seashore.

Yang had accompanied them at a distance to ensure they made it onto the bus.

That had been at 0805. Over an hour ago. Bolan felt his cell phone vibrate and checked the incoming text. It was from Yang.

On board. Come get me.

"Swing by and pick her up," Bolan said.

"Okay, boss," Herbie said with a lopsided grin, a cigarette dancing between his lips as he talked.

Bolan still wasn't certain how trustworthy this guy was, and that was why he wanted to keep Yang with them as they proceeded to part two: getting Sammo Han out of harm's way. After Tressman had been taken out of Song Jing he'd feigned ignorance when the PLA soldiers had ordered him about in Mandarin, making them resort to gestures and shoves. Right before the deuce-and-a-half had been ambushed, Tressman had overheard two soldiers say that Sammo Han was to be formally taken into custody later this morning. That meant the evac plan had to be put into overdrive. Bolan still wasn't sure how they were going to accomplish all this now that they were without their helicopter. He hadn't even seen Han's house up close.

"That Yang's kind of a hot number," Grimaldi said as they approached the bus station. "I wonder if I'll have time to show her a little bit of the Chinese nightclub scene before we ship out?"

"Just make sure you stay on the right side of the road," Bolan said. He tapped Herbie's shoulder and pointed to Yang, who was walking briskly toward the corner. "Pull ahead of her and I'll open the door."

"Okay, boss."

When she got into the front passenger seat Yang smiled, but she still looked nervous. "They all got on the bus."

"Good," Bolan said. "Now let's go pick up Sammo Han and get out of here. Does that Tai Pang guy Tressman told us about speak English?"

"I don't know for sure," Yang said. "Tressman was the only one who dealt with him. I don't even know what he looks like."

"What about you, Herbie?" Bolan asked. "You know this guy, Tai Pang?"

Herbie shook his head, causing ash to drop from his cigarette. "I never see him."

Bolan handed Yang the phone number Tressman had given him. "Call him and tell him we need to set up a meet after we get Han."

Yang nodded and made the call.

Bolan reviewed his options. The simplest plan would be to grab the lawyer, head for the American embassy and have him ask for political asylum. But from what Tressman and Huang had said, Bolan doubted Han would go for that unless his wife and granddaughter were already safely out of the country. The next best move would be to get him out of Beijing. The capital was too hot, and the Chinese were too efficient at shutting everything down if they were searching for somebody, especially a couple of Americans who'd been involved in a shooting incident. Bolan and Grimaldi could be on the most-wanted list already.

Yang held her hand over the cell phone and turned to him. "He wants to know what your plan is."

"Tell him we'll let him know at the meet," Bolan said. "Just set up a time and we'll call him back with the place."

She nodded and relayed the message in Mandarin into the cell phone.

"Why am I starting to feel like that little Dutch boy?" Grimaldi asked. "Sticking our fingers in the holes in the dike, just hoping it all don't come crashing over us."

"You'd have a hard time passing for Dutch." Bolan grinned. "But I'd like to catch a glimpse of you in those wooden shoes."

SAMMO HAN LIVED in a modern-looking area composed of row after row of white, four-story town houses with balconies. Decorative wrought iron fences surrounded each complex, and a narrow walkway ran behind each group of houses, bordered by a six-foot-high wall on each side. The neighborhood was set along an asphalt street that stretched into the distance. In a picture, it could have been Anyplace, USA, but it was on the outskirts of Beijing. Tall skyscrapers loomed in the distance.

Bolan thought about the disparity between this scene and the one from last night. China was obviously doing a lot of upgrading, but he'd also heard the dichotomy between the urban rich and the rural poor was more pronounced the farther you got from the cities.

They drove slowly past a section of houses that looked virtually identical to the ones on the last block, except the house in the middle had a contingent of uniformed soldiers standing in front of it. Four men stood smoking cigarettes, their QBZ-95 rifles slung across their chests. Bolan told Herbie to drive on past.

"Does Han speak English?" Bolan asked.

"Yes," Yang said.

"Those houses have a rear entrance?" Grimaldi asked. "There's nothing like a good old Chicago-style alley for sneaking somebody out the back door."

"No alleys here," Bolan said. "Just walkways."

He turned to Yang. "Do you think Han will go with us willingly?"

She shrugged. "Originally, he just wanted us to take his family out. He was adamant about staying, but that was before we knew he was going to be arrested this morning. I think he'll play ball."

"If he doesn't," Grimaldi said, "I say we leave him to his own resources and beat feet outta here."

"That's not an option," Bolan said. "Hal said Han's got some special information regarding that deal I broke up between the Triad and the Iranians."

Grimaldi sighed. "Well, that's good to know." His eyebrows rose and he pointed. "What the— Will you look at that?"

A convoy of vans followed a black Mercedes limousine down the block. The vans all had huge folded antennas on their roofs. Most of the lettering on the sides was Chinese, but a few of them spelled out CNN.

"Any idea what this is about?" Bolan asked.

Yang compressed her lips for a moment, then said, "I'll bet it's J. Michael Major. He's over here attending the sporting events and made a big point of saying he was going to meet with Sammo Han."

"J. Michael Major?" Grimaldi said. "The actor?"

"The Midnight Crusader himself," Yang replied. "He's big on human rights issues. He even started a special school in Kenya for girls who've been abused."

"Maybe we can use this to our advantage," Bolan said. "It looks like some Western reporters are here. If we're seen, we won't stand out so much."

"We're not exactly dressed for the occasion," Grimaldi said, holding his hand in front of his black BDU shirt.

"Herbie, drop Yang and me off over there," Bolan said as he slipped off his own BDU shirt and shoulder rig and set them on the floor next to Grimaldi. "Keep an eye on everything for me." He cocked his head fractionally at Herbie.

Grimaldi nodded and grinned. "I can't believe you're leaving your baby with me. I feel honored."

"I can't think of a better babysitter," Bolan said, wishing he had a second gun to take along, just in case. "I'll call you when we're ready to be picked up."

The van pulled to a stop and Bolan jumped out, followed by the young woman. They cut through some side yards, walking down the narrow lane that separated one set of houses from another. When they got to Han's house, Bolan stopped and reconnoitered a bit. He was able to steal a quick look over the high wall. Two soldiers in Han's backyard were standing by the side of the house craning their necks to get a view of the activity in front. Both men had QBZ-95 rifles.

Bolan waited, pondering his next move. He motioned

to Yang to move to the next house. He boosted her over the wall and they made their way through the adjacent yard. A white picket fence separated the two yards then ended abruptly, allowing for a small shared courtyard. Bolan and Yang moved quickly. The soldier, who was still focused on the scene in front, didn't notice them. The area in between the houses was a narrow twelve feet, but was obscured by shadows.

Close enough to shake hands with your neighbor, Bolan thought. They moved to the edge of the building and saw a Caucasian man clad in a black leather jacket on the street moving toward the front of Han's house. The man's hair was feathered back and his face had a chiseled, handsome cast. A gaggle of reporters and cameramen followed him.

"That's J. Michael Major," Yang whispered.

Bolan nodded. "You think the soldiers will let him inside?"

"I doubt it. The Politburo's already said they won't tolerate any of the Western press giving a forum to troublemakers."

As if in response, two of the soldiers in front immediately sprang forward, holding their rifles at port arms and shouting.

"They're ordering him to stop," Yang said.

Major continued, his movements imbued with a cocky swagger. The soldiers shouted again. The reporters and cameramen fanned out, stepping back slightly as they recorded every movement. The soldiers moved in front of the advancing movie star. He stopped, flashed a Hollywood smile, and stood with his hands on his hips.

"I'm J. Michael Major," the movie star announced in his stentorian voice, "and I'm here to see Han Son Chi, also known as Sammo Han."

One of the soldiers shouted something in Mandarin.

Major flashed his high wattage grin again. "Sorry, I don't understand. Are you welcoming me?"

He stepped forward and the soldier made a quick movement with his rifle, knocking the movie star backward. Suddenly four new police vehicles, lights and sirens blaring, whirled around the corner. They skidded to a halt and a small army of uniformed police spilled out. One officer, with a cluster of silver diamonds on his epaulets, began blowing a whistle and shouting commands.

Two cops moved toward Major.

"Hey, you dare to touch me," the actor was shouting, "and it'll be on every television network in the world and the internet before noon."

One of the cops in the background leaned over and whispered into the commander's ear.

Two of the cops stepped up holding nightsticks.

"Listen," Major yelled, "do you know who I am? I played the Midnight Crusader in my last movie. I make more money in one movie than all of you put together will make in a hundred years."

"This might be the diversion we need," Bolan said, steering Yang toward the back of the house. He placed a hand on her shoulder. "Give me your weapon."

Her eyes widened. "You're going to shoot them? The guards, I mean."

Bolan didn't answer. He didn't want to kill the rear sentries. The men were soldiers doing their job, and they weren't a direct threat as of yet. Plus, the sound of a couple of shots from the Walther would no doubt alert the group in front. But on the other hand, he didn't want to face two armed men without being able to return fire if necessary.

As they moved along the side of the house Bolan heard two snicking sounds, like sharp pops cutting through the air. He recognized them immediately as reports from a sound-suppressed pistol. He thrust his arm across Yang's chest, knocking her back against the side of the house.

"Hey!" she yelled.

"Shh," Bolan said as he pushed her to a squatting position. They were about ten feet from the edge of the house.

Bolan heard voices, the sound of breaking glass and then the burst of wood.

Sounds as if they're going inside, he thought.

He shifted the Walther to his left hand and withdrew the Espada knife with his right, flicking open the long blade. Edging toward the corner, he was suddenly confronted by a Triad hit man holding a Norinco Type 54 with a long sound suppressor attached. Bolan reached forward and smashed the man's right wrist with the Walther. As the weapon dropped out of the would-be assailant's hand, Bolan pivoted and drove the Espada into the man's gut and pushed upward. The hit man gasped, blood seeping out of his mouth. Bolan quickly pulled him around the corner and threw him to the ground. He wiped his blade on the man's pants leg, refolded the knife and put it back into his pocket. As he turned to pick up the fallen Norinco he saw that Yang was in the process of throwing up. He squatted beside her.

"Are you all right?"

She nodded, then vomited again. Bolan handed her the Walther and grabbed the Norinco. He pulled the slide back a fraction to make sure there was a round in the chamber and saw the shiny brass casing.

Moving to the corner again, he took a quick look.

The yard was empty except for the bodies of the two sentries, both of whom lay prone with expanding puddles of crimson around their heads. They still had their rifles slung. Whoever had killed them hadn't been interested in retrieving the bulky weapons. That most likely meant they were already armed and wanted to move fast. Bolan knew he had to move fast, as well. He turned to Yang.

"Looks like the Triad's going after Sammo Han," he whispered. "Follow my lead and don't shoot unless you have to. Ready?"

The young woman wiped her mouth and nodded.

She has some pluck, Bolan thought.

They both stood up and began cautiously moving. Bolan motioned for her to stop a few feet from the corner as he stepped back, raised the silenced Norinco, and began to edge around the corner, exposing as little of himself as possible while retaining the ability to get off a quick shot. The rear door had been broken open and hung loosely from its hinges. Inside, he heard a low, guttural voice speaking in Mandarin and caught a glimpse of three men, all clad in black leather jackets and wraparound sunglasses, standing around a fourth man who was on his knees. He was missing his left arm. One of the standing men was holding a knife against the kneeling man's cheekbone. He yelled down at him.

"Can you understand him?" Bolan whispered to Yang.

She nodded. "He said, 'Where's the dragon key?'"

Bolan filed this information for later and positioned himself along the edge of the doorjamb. He pointed the Norinco at the head of the man holding the knife, allowing for the sight-obscuring upper rim and extra weight of the sound suppressor. He squeezed the trigger. The man's head jerked, leaving a mist of red as he twisted and fell. Bolan zeroed in on the other two hit men, shooting the second one in the base of the neck as he turned and catching the third one with two rounds in the chest. The man on the floor looked toward Bolan with an expression of horror as the Executioner moved with quick strides through the house.

"Mr. Han," Bolan said, "we're here to help you." He continued to sweep the rooms, checking for other assailants, but found none. "Anybody else here?"

The man's jaw dropped slightly, then he shook his head.

Yang came in and started talking to Han in Mandarin. Bolan went to the front windows and peered through a lace curtain. Outside, a group of people milled about, gesturing at the house and shouting in Mandarin and English. A couple police officers pushed the actor back as the news cameras recorded everything. One of the police officials glanced at the scene and said something. A group of officers approached the cameramen and another struggle started. Bolan went back to Yang and Han, who was now on his feet. A trail of crimson dripped from a cut on his cheek.

"We've got to get out of here." Bolan turned to Yang. "Call Herbie and tell him to pick us up where he dropped us."

She nodded and took out her cell phone.

Han shook his head. "I cannot go. I must stay."

"In another minute they'll be coming inside." Bolan gestured at the three dead men. "These guys were Triad, so they're gunning for you now. Plus there are two dead PLA soldiers out back. You think you'll be able to explain your way out of all this?"

Han blinked twice, then nodded. "You are right, of

course." He pointed to a harness and prosthesis lying on the nearby table. "But I will need that."

Bolan grabbed it and headed for the door. "Let's go. Now."

Han grabbed a jacket and smiled. "I am very glad that at least, I could give you a hand."

Bolan glanced at the prosthesis and grinned.

8

After lifting Yang and Han over the six-foot concrete wall at the rear of the property, Bolan tucked the Norinco into the left side of his belt and scaled the wall himself. He landed lightly in the narrow walkway between the houses and motioned for the others to follow him toward the adjacent street where he hoped Herbie and Grimaldi would be waiting. Han, who was carrying his artificial left arm in his right hand, was having trouble keeping up. Bolan slowed his pace and looked around. No one seemed to be following them, but it was only a matter of time before the police found the bodies and started closing things down and doing a house-to-house, vehicle-by-vehicle search. They had to be out of there before that.

He glanced over his shoulder. Han was walking now, his artificial arm dragging on the ground next to him.

Bolan pivoted and started running back to him. Yang slowed when she saw him, but he motioned for her to continue and went to Han.

"Mr. Han, what's the problem? You having trouble keeping up?"

Han smiled wanly. "I regret my tardiness, but my stomach is very sore. When those gangsters accosted me in my home, they hit me numerous times." He took two more steps and stopped. "I can go no farther. I am sorry."

"We can't wait," Bolan said. "I'll carry you." He bent his legs, flipped Han over his left shoulder and began sprinting toward the end of the walkway. He caught up to Yang at the mouth of the alleyway and scanned the street for the van. It was nowhere in sight.

"Call Herbie back," Bolan said. "See what the problem is."

She took out her cell phone and hit the call button.

"Are you going to put me down now or carry me all the way out of Beijing?" Han asked.

Bolan gently lowered the man's feet to the ground and apologized.

Han grinned. "No need to say you're sorry. You are very big and very strong."

Yang turned to Bolan. "He says he's almost here."

Bolan nodded and did another scan of the area. A few people were on the street, heading toward the growing brouhaha in front of Han's house. Hopefully, it would last a few more minutes and give them the chance to escape notice. But that also meant remaining as inconspicuous as possible.

"Mr. Han," Bolan said, "this would be a good time to put on your arm. It'll make you less noticeable."

"It is a rather laborious procedure," Han said. "And I will need to buy a new shirt." He was clad in a T-shirt that made his missing limb even more conspicuous. "But please, call me Sammo. That is my English name."

"Okay, Sammo. Can you just hold it across your body for the time being?"

Han nodded and held the arm against his left side. "And what is your name?"

"You can call me Matt Cooper," Bolan said.

Han nodded. "Ah, a man such as yourself must have many names. Am I correct, Cooper-*jun?*"

Bolan didn't answer. He heard the high whine of an engine and turned to see the van accelerating down the street. Herbie had been true to his word. After another quick glance, Bolan told Yang and Han to walk at a normal pace toward the street. Running at this point would only draw attention. The van screeched to a stop at the curb.

So much for being inconspicuous.

Grimaldi slid the side door open and helped Yang and Han inside. Bolan got in last and slammed the door shut.

"We need to get out of here fast," he said. "But try not to make it look like we robbed a bank."

"Gotcha, boss," Herbie said. He executed an arcing U-turn and bounced up and over a curb and a grass parkway. Then he accelerated toward the main roadway.

"Slow it down," Bolan said.

Herbie was lighting another cigarette as he drove. "Everybody in China drive fast."

Bolan caught a glimpse of the man's lopsided grin in the rearview mirror.

"No sweat, boss," Herbie said. "Me number one driver."

There was no alternative at the moment, but Bolan made a mental note that their exodus from Beijing would not be by truck, van or automobile. The simplest plan would be to head to the American embassy and try to smuggle Han inside. Then he could ask for political asylum. But it wasn't quite that simple. For one thing, the Chinese were already looking for Tressman, an escaped American spy, so they most likely had the embassy staked out, perhaps even surrounded.

If they could get to the coast, and buy or steal a boat, Brognola would arrange a Navy pickup somewhere on the Yellow Sea. That had been Tressman's original plan. But this was an immense country and the drive would be at least eight to ten hours. Perhaps there was a better way.

He turned to Yang. "You have Tai Pang's number?"

She nodded.

Bolan was more than a little concerned that this asset had been compromised when Tressman was interrogated. But if that were the case, the Chinese would have probably already picked him up. They had to move quickly, and Tressman's original plan was out the window. "We need transportation out of here. Beijing's too hot."

"You want me to call him?" she asked. "Where do we want to go?"

"Just find the number for now."

Bolan considered their options. Hong Kong would be his first choice. He had more contacts there, but it was also the farthest destination and pretty much out of their reach unless they could somehow get on an airplane. The chances of that were slim to none. Tressman and Han's family were en route to Shandong Province on the coast, which was about five or six hundred kilometers away. That was a more logical departure point.

"Herbie," Bolan said, "how long will it take us to get to Shandong?"

Herbie blew out a plume of smoke as he took the cigarette out of his mouth. "Shandong, no problem. Some good road, some bad. Maybe five, six hour."

"Let's go for it," Bolan said.

Han put his hand on Bolan's arm. "Cooper-*jun,* I am sorry," he said. "But I must first go to Shanghai."

"Shanghai? That's twice as far. And your family's heading to Shandong."

Han shook his head. "Mr. Tressman told me he had their departure ensured. I must go to Shanghai."

"You planning on seeing the fight?" Grimaldi asked.

Han looked puzzled, then smiled. "Ah, Zhang Won Yu, the Olympian."

Grimaldi nodded. "Good amateur record. Something like three hundred and fifty fights, right?"

Han smiled. "I am sorry. I know of him, but I do not follow boxing."

He turned to Bolan. "I have an item of supreme importance that I must pick up in Shanghai before I leave China."

Bolan remembered the conversation back at Han's house. "The dragon key?"

Han's eyes widened, then he nodded. "You know much, Cooper-*jun*. And if you know about the dragon key, you know its importance and why we must visit Shanghai."

Although it was more than seven hundred kilometers farther than Shandong Province, Shanghai afforded some other advantages. With the big boxing match only two days away, there would be a lot of Westerners in the city. He and Grimaldi wouldn't stand out as much, and they could use their cover story as sports journalists if they were stopped. The best place to hide was in plain sight. Plus, if they could get to the American Consulate in Shanghai, it could smooth the way for them to make a quick exit out of China.

"Herbie, besides flying, what's the fastest way to get to Shanghai from here?"

Herbie drew on his cigarette, then tossed the butt out

the window. "Bullet train. Get you there in four hour forty-eight minute."

Han tugged at his sleeve. "We will need tickets in advance. And you must have a Chinese ID card to purchase them."

"Hopefully, we've got that covered," Bolan said, as he took out a stack of yuan and turned to Yang. "Call Tai Pang and tell him we'll need five bullet train tickets. We'll meet him at Beijing South Railway Station in thirty minutes."

"Tickets to Shanghai?" she asked.

"No, tell him we're going to Hong Kong."

Han started to say something, but Bolan raised his finger to his lips and shook his head.

BEIJING SOUTH RAILWAY Station was an immense, domed structure of glass and metal between the second and third ring roads. Bolan told Herbie to take one trip around it so they could get their bearings. He slipped off his BDU shirt and set it, the Beretta and the shoulder rig on top of his bag. After slipping into a nondescript blue shirt, he grabbed Grimaldi's fancy suitcase and tossed it on the seat next to him.

"Hey," Grimaldi said, "that's a Louis Vuitton original."

"Exactly," Bolan replied, patting the bottom. The designer bag had a hollow section lined with a mesh of lead filaments that were designed to obscure x-ray examinations. "While Yang and I check things out and get the tickets, you disassemble our weapons and stow them in this finely crafted piece of French luggage."

"Ah, I have it on good authority that the French use only the finest *Italian* leather," Grimaldi said.

"Oh, forget the finely crafted part, then," Bolan said with a grin. "Herbie, let us off over there."

"Okay, boss. No problem." He steered the van to the curb and stopped near the edge of the south entrance.

Bolan took out his Espada knife, handed it to Grimaldi, and told Yang to give him her gun, as well.

"See if you can fit this one in there, too," he said. "If not, leave it in the van."

"Why?" Yang asked.

"We'll be under tight scrutiny from here," Bolan said. "Unless you have a special place to hide it, we can't take the chance it'll be found."

She nodded and handed the gun over.

Grimaldi looked at the small Walther and shrugged. "I'll see what I can do."

"I can put part of it in my arm," Han said. He tapped the prosthesis. "I have plenty of extra room in here. Lots of big muscles."

Bolan grinned. He was starting to like this man.

He opened the door and slid out, followed by Yang, and they strolled along the huge sidewalk leading to the entrance. Four huge red Chinese characters were affixed to the crest of the metal dome, and *Beijing South Railway Station* was spelled out in English on a secondary tier below.

"Where's this guy supposed to meet us?"

"There's a large waiting area on the second level," she said. "He said to go to the fifth set of chairs and wait there. He'll contact us when he's sure it's safe."

Bolan didn't like it but knew he had little choice. It was the perfect place for a setup. He hoped Tressman had chosen his asset well. "Any idea what this guy looks like?"

She shook her head. "He goes by the code name of Tai Pang, which means overweight, if that helps."

"Does he speak English?"

She shrugged again. "Sorry, I forgot to ask. We only spoke in Mandarin."

This gets better and better, Bolan thought as they made their way to the upward escalators. He scanned the surrounding area as they ascended. Meeting an unknown entity was always tricky, but on the plus side, the station was so immense and densely populated that they stood out less. There were also a substantial number of Westerners milling about, but most were in groups. Huge television screens affixed to the wall on his right displayed arrival and departure times with colorful characters and numerals. Glancing upward, he saw multiple tinted globes suspended at various levels from the ceiling. Pan-tilt-and-zoom cameras. Somebody was watching.

The second level had a series of ticket booths flanked by endless rows of red couches. He counted off the five sections from the escalators and went to that row. There was one seat left and as awkward as he felt taking it and leaving Yang standing, he sat down.

"Sorry for not being a gentleman," he said, "but I figured I'd be less noticeable this way."

"That's okay." She smiled. "I like tall men."

Bolan opened a newspaper he'd picked up and held it in front of him. Hopefully, it would provide some cover from the ubiquitous camera lenses. He caught sight of one of the opaque bulbs on the ceiling and adjusted the paper accordingly.

Yeah, he thought. This affords about as much protection as a baseball cap in a thunderstorm.

Yang's cell phone chimed with an incoming text. She looked at it and said, "It's him. He's using pinyin."

"Pin what?"

"English letters to spell out the Mandarin phonetically."

Bolan nodded. He'd heard the Chinese were becoming a nation of poor spellers due to their fascination for texting.

Another thing old Mao would despise, he thought.

"He says he'll need passports and Chinese ID cards to get all the tickets," she said.

Bolan had anticipated such a development. It would necessitate abandoning the van, bringing the rest of the group inside and bunching themselves together. He thought about telling this Tai Pang guy to shove off, but the clock was still ticking and he didn't know how much longer it would be before the Chinese started a widespread search for Han and his American helpers.

"All right," Bolan said, "but tell him I want to meet first. On the lower level."

She thumbed in the message and waited for a reply.

"He says okay."

"Ask how we'll know him," Bolan said.

She thumbed another text, waited again, then said, "He'll approach us and ask for a light for his cigarette."

Bolan nodded, folded the newspaper and got up. As he headed for the escalator he noticed a man staring at him. As Bolan's eyes met his, the man looked away. Was this Tai Pang? Bolan continued to the escalator with Yang. The man followed, getting on the down escalator behind a group of Chinese. Bolan turned to talk to Yang, pointing at the far end of the massive foyer at a decorative statute, and whispered, "I think we picked up a tail."

She smiled and nodded, gazing at the statue.

As they descended, Bolan saw the man talking on a cell phone. He was wearing a dark jacket, and Bolan noticed a slight bulge on the right side, along the guy's belt. He was armed. The man's dark eyes settled on Bolan and stayed there. There was no subterfuge or evasiveness this time. Either this guy was Tai Pang or he was an undercover cop. Bolan decided it was the latter as he saw three more good-size men standing at the base of the escalator. The bulges under their jackets indicated they were cops as well, unless Tai Pang had brought along his own protection squad.

Bolan turned and whispered, "Looks like we've got a reception party waiting for us."

Yang's mouth pulled into a thin line. "What'll we do?"

"Maybe they're just after me. You keep walking while I draw their attention. Try to get back to our van and get out of here."

"But—"

"No buts."

"Okay," she said.

The three men at the bottom flanked both sides of the escalator. As the people immediately in front of them stepped off, one of the men flashed some sort of wallet with a badge and ID card. He said something in Mandarin.

Bolan cocked his head back and smiled as he stepped off to the side to let Yang slip through. "I'm sorry, I don't speak Chinese."

"But I'm sure your little friend does," the man behind them said. He barked an order and the three bigger guys held out their arms, preventing Yang from moving toward the exits.

"We are the police," the first guy said. "Walk this way."

Bolan debated his options. He might be able to take out all four of them quick enough to give Yang and him a chance to make a run for it, but as he glanced toward the doors he saw a uniformed police officer standing by the exit with a submachine gun slung casually over his shoulder.

"Over there," the man said, pointing toward a solid door in the rear wall.

"What's this about?" Bolan asked. "I just asked this girl to help me get a ticket. I don't know her."

"Is that so? You came in together. You were talking together. And I did not see you make any attempt to purchase a ticket."

Bolan frowned. This was going from bad to worse in a hurry.

One of the other cops produced a key and shoved it into the slot above the doorknob. He twisted it and opened the door.

"Go in there," the man said. "To the office."

Bolan started down a deserted corridor, heading to the door at the other end. A set of large windows was on the wall to his left, revealing a small room with a chair and a table. If he waited until they were all in the corridor, he'd have a good chance at a counterstrike that was outside the public view.

The lead cop must have assumed that, too, because as Bolan glanced back he saw a pistol in the officer's hand.

"A gun?" Bolan said. "Is that really necessary?"

The man smiled. "It is until I determine it is not." The smile faded. "Now go into that room and tell me what your business is here." He pointed the weapon at Bolan. "You will get on your knees. Both of you."

Yang glanced at him, a look of distress on her face.

The man shoved her. Bolan turned, but the officer pointed the gun straight at him, staying just out of Bolan's reach. He had no way to retaliate without putting Yang in harm's way. One of the other big men opened the door, stepped inside and motioned them in. They walked into the room.

"Get on your knees!" the man shouted.

Bolan was starting to kneel, assessing his chances for a desperate leap to grab the gun, when he heard shouting in the hallway outside. Yang's brow furrowed as she glanced at him.

More shouting came from the hallway, intertwined with what sounded like a happy drunk. Another man had appeared, a smile stretched across his face. He was dressed in a blue jacket and was much shorter than the two huge cops. The drunken man mumbled something and two of the cops shouted at him. The drunk laughed and staggered toward them, singing an off-key song. He held up his hand, displaying a glass bottle with a Chinese label. Bolan recognized it as cheap wine.

One of the big cops reached for the drunk, who ducked nimbly out of the way, wagging his finger and smiling. The big cop snarled and reached out with both hands. In a flash, the drunk delivered a snapping kick to the cop's throat. His hands immediately went to his neck and the drunk's foot whipped up, scythe-like, and caught the second cop on the temple. He crumpled.

The drunk was at the doorjamb now, the bottle flying from his hand. It soared across the room and struck the cop with the gun in the face. Bolan reached up and snatched the gun from the man's grasp.

The drunk thrust a vertical kick to the neck of the cop lying in the hallway and stepped forward, delivering another quick, chopping blow to the throat of the fourth police officer. That man fell to the floor.

The cop who'd been struck by the bottle staggered to his feet, glanced around and began pulling a radio from a pouch on his belt. The drunk delivered a hooking heel kick to the cop's face that knocked him against the wall. In the next instant, the drunk was back on the balls of his feet, a silver blade gleaming in his right hand.

A *balisong,* Bolan thought.

The blade flashed with a forward thrust and the cop's throat was suddenly torn open, his eyes wide with terror as he fell.

Bolan raised the captured pistol and pointed it at the drunk, who stopped and stared at him with dark, foreboding eyes.

"Don't move," Bolan said in Mandarin.

"I do not think you wish to do that," the drunk said in almost perfectly accented English. "Not if you wish to leave Beijing, as per our agreement."

Bolan kept the gun pointed at the stranger.

"Or," the stranger said, "would you rather I ask you for a light?" He made a quick movement, bouncing the blade against the back of his hand and then flipping it so it retracted back into the handle. He paused and slipped the knife into his pocket.

Bolan canted his head, but said nothing.

The man's mouth edged into a slight smile. "I am Tai Pang. Now, if you wish to continue with our planned departure, you must assist me in placing these bodies where they will not be found."

Bolan lowered the pistol and looked the guy up and down. "You're Tai Pang?"

The man nodded.

"Funny," Bolan said, "you don't look overweight."

9

As he waited in the long hallway, replete with vases of flowers and finely crafted bronze statuettes, General Wong continued to feel the vague rumblings in his bowels. Being called before the Standing Committee for the second time in two days was not pleasant. This time he would have even more questions to answer, especially in view of the recent blunders by the squad of soldiers he'd dispatched to pick up Tressman.

He could blame the foreigners for that debacle, but Wong had selected the soldiers. The escape of Han would no doubt be brought up, as well. Two incidents, back-to-back, in which his soldiers had ended up looking like amateurs. At least partial blame for this second incident could be shared with the police.

In theory, as a respected, decorated PLA officer, he should be beyond reproach. Wong had proved himself in Tiananmen Square. He'd been one of the first officers to order his men to fire on the troublemakers. Certainly that should count for something with the Standing Committee, even if the incident itself had been downplayed in recent years. But who knew what those old, senile whoresons really thought? He sighed.

If only he had that damn dragon key. He could be making arrangements to get out of China for good. Chen assured him that the dragon key would be recovered, but so far the quest had proved as elusive as trying to trap a cloud of smoke.

The door opened and a uniformed soldier stepped out, snapped to attention and announced that the Committee was ready to see him.

Wong straightened his uniform before he walked into the room. As he made his way up the long aisle toward the benches, he noticed the figure of another man standing erect and proper in his navy uniform. As Wong got closer he saw who it was: Colonel Yeoung of the National Police.

The bastard was called in first, Wong thought, so they could grill him before they talked to me.

The rumbling in his bowels took an upsurge. He needed a cigarette to calm himself, but dared not smoke in the presence of the Committee. Such an act would be seen as a measure of disrespect. He tightened his sphincter muscle and held himself ramrod straight.

He stopped at the lectern and stood at attention, announcing himself with pride and precision. "General Wong Su Tong of the People's Liberation Army reporting as ordered."

The old men looked down at him from their elevated positions without saying a word. Finally, Minister Cao, the one in the center who oversaw matters of internal security, spoke.

"General, we ordered you to bring the American spy here, did we not?"

"Yes, Minister." Wong felt like he was being jabbed with a stick.

"Then why is he not here?" The old prick smiled. He was obviously enjoying this.

"I sent a contingent of men to assume custody of

the American and transport him here, Minister." Wong paused. His mouth felt dry. "Unfortunately, the squad was ambushed. My men were killed, and the American was taken from them."

"So we have heard," Cao said. The old fool removed a cigarette from his gold case, tapped it lightly on the metallic surface and lit it with an ornamental lighter. "We will now hear your explanation of this failure."

They show me no respect, Wong thought. He gathered himself, wondering what Yeoung had told them. He decided to stick to his original plan.

"We are waiting, General." Cao held his cigarette to his lips and drew deeply on it. As he exhaled the smoke he stared down at Wong with a reproachful look. "How do you account for this ambush, as you call it? This failure?"

Wong had to tread carefully here. To suggest that the details of the plan had been leaked from within the Committee would be construed as a massive insult. There were only two other possible explanations. Wong did not want to name himself as one of them, so he did the next best thing.

"I have it on good authority that there is a traitor employed at Song Jing Prison. I was going to contact the National Police to investigate." He paused and glanced at the uniformed man standing to his left. "But since Colonel Yeoung is already standing before you, I shall refer the information to him. I lost four men due to this treachery."

Cao brought the cigarette to his lips once again, looking from Wong to Yeoung.

He holds the damn thing like a woman, Wong thought.

"A traitor? Do you know who was responsible for this, Colonel?" Cao asked.

"No, esteemed Minister," Colonel Yeoung said. "I shall launch an immediate investigation and report back to you."

Cao nodded, smiled and drew on his cigarette again. Wong could almost taste the smoke.

"General," Cao said, "you were also instructed to bring Han Son Chu before us, were you not?"

"Yes, most esteemed Minister," Wong said.

Cao smiled. The old fool loved to have men of authority fawn all over him.

"Yet," Cao said, "you failed to accomplish this, as well. What is your explanation?"

"As you instructed, I placed a guard on the trouble-maker's house but told my men to wait until the American movie star and the news media had gone before formally arresting Han and bringing him here."

Cao nodded, smiled again.

"I lost two more men at this scene," Wong said. He cocked his head toward Colonel Yeoung. "The National Police were also on the scene in full force. They were engaged in a dispute with the movie star, and by the time order was restored, Han was gone."

"Colonel Yeoung." Cao took one last drag then stubbed the cigarette out in an ashtray. "Do you know who is responsible for this?"

"The bodies of four men were recovered from the house," Yeoung said. "It is believed that the trouble-maker is being assisted by traitors within our own citizenry."

"Traitors?" Cao said, raising his eyebrows.

"Gangsters," Yeoung answered. "I believe the Triads may be involved." Yeoung went into a long-winded explanation of his investigation and concluded by saying he had not yet come to any firm conclusions.

"You investigate, and yet neither Han nor the American spy have been located." Cao picked up his gold cigarette case. "Do you have anything further to report on this matter?"

Wong felt a surge of relief. They seemed to be concentrating on Yeoung's failures.

As Yeoung was replying with more double-talk, Wong had an idea.

"Most esteemed Minister," he said. "It has also come to my attention that four transit police operatives were murdered this morning at Beijing South Railway Station. I believe this is connected to the previous two incidents."

The news got Cao's attention. Yeoung had most likely briefed the Committee on the incident, but by bringing it up, Wong gave the appearance of being on top of things.

Cao focused his attention on Wong and smiled. "And on what evidence do you base that assumption?"

"I have no direct evidence," Wong said, "other than the report that an American was involved in the incident at Beijing South, as well."

"I see," Cao said as he took another cigarette out of the case and closed it with a snap. "Colonel Yeoung, you mentioned that you've discovered which train the suspects are now on."

"Yes, most esteemed Minister," Yeoung said. "We have traced the purchase they made."

That cowardly bastard stole my "most esteemed Minister" line, Wong thought.

"Very well, then," Cao said. "Perhaps you and General Wong can work together." He put the cigarette between his lips and held the lighter to the tip. "General, send a detachment of troops to stop that train and take custody of the Americans and the troublemaker." He exhaled a plume of smoke, then fixed both of them with a baleful stare. "Do you each feel confident that you can accomplish that task?"

"Yes, most esteemed Minister," Wong replied, gritting his teeth as Yeoung echoed his words.

BOLAN HAD TO admit the Chinese bullet trains looked impressive. They had a sleek engine that resembled a rocket ship, and their cruising speed was listed as 186 miles per hour. Taking one of those would have gotten them to Shanghai a lot quicker than the Class D sleeper train they'd ended up riding, but now they had their own deluxe private compartment with two pull-down bunks and a bathroom. It was turning out to be a convenient way of keeping a low profile.

After hiding the bodies in a maintenance closet at the Beijing South Railway Station, Bolan shelled out enough yuan to buy six first-class tickets on the bullet train to Hong Kong. Then Bolan had Herbie and Tai Pang do some informal horse-trading to exchange them for six tickets on the sleeper to Shanghai while Yang listened in.

Once the slain officers were found, the authorities would pull out all the stops to trace the purchases. Switching trains and locations on the black market would buy them a little extra time. Still, Bolan harbored no illusions about how much of an edge this would give them. Once the false trail had been discovered, the Chinese could stop each and every train that had departed Beijing until they found the right one. But that was a lot of ground to cover, even with a two-million-man army.

Herbie hadn't been too keen on abandoning his van,

but Bolan told Grimaldi to tell him they'd buy him a brand-new one. So he'd left it in a tow-away zone and helped carry the luggage into the train station. Leaving Herbie behind wasn't an option. The Beijing slickster had proved useful thus far, but he was still a mercenary.

Bolan felt only slightly better about his latest associate. Tressman would've vetted Tai Pang, but the man had shown no hesitation jumping into the fray, which a government agent would not do. One thing was for sure, the guy was extremely skilled in martial arts, and totally ruthless. He'd dispatched four police officers in the railway station without blinking an eye. Well, not quite. Bolan had detected a slight flickering of the man's right eyelid before he struck. Whether it was a reliable way to forecast an attack remained to be seen. Bolan hoped he wouldn't have occasion to find out.

The train jolted slightly and he swayed with the movement. Grimaldi, who was snoring on the upper bunk, murmured something in his sleep. Herbie sat dozing in one corner, and Yang slumbered in the opposite one. Bolan looked at Tai Pang. The slender Chinese man was sitting in a lotus position on the floor, staring back at Bolan. The guy never seemed to get tired or bored.

"How about going to the diner car and getting us all some food?" Bolan said.

Tai Pang nodded. Without another word he got to his feet and left.

Bolan went to the door and locked it after him, wondering what was the real story behind Tai Pang. But there was no way Bolan could contact Tressman to ask him anything.

THE MANTIS PAUSED in the gangway and looked out the window, watching the countryside fly by in the evening gloom. This was not the first time he'd taken a train between cities, but the swaying movement and flashing scenery never ceased to fascinate him. And then there was the sheen of the cars themselves. He ran his fingers over a chrome door. The Mantis liked shiny things.

He assumed this affinity was the result of his deprived childhood. He remembered the orphanage on the outskirts of Hong Kong. Even while guarding his younger sister, he would continually rub his small fingers over every shiny surface he saw, hoping that coins would magically spring forth. He reached inside his pants pocket and rubbed his fingers over the shiny surface of the stainless-steel pistol he'd taken from the British agent. It was a souvenir, but one that held little intrinsic value, as he seldom used guns. Prudence dictated that he discard it, but his inner voice told him to hold on to it for the moment.

Such reverie was superfluous. He needed to give an update to Master Chen. His mission was still incomplete, and if he wanted to feel those shiny coins in his hands, he must keep on track. An apt metaphor for a man on a train. He smiled. The Mantis pressed the button on his cell phone.

Master Chen answered immediately. "I have been hoping you would call me. All is well?"

"It is. Everything is proceeding according to our calculations."

"Have you located the item yet?"

"No," the Mantis said. "He has secreted it in Shanghai."

"I see that you are proceeding there now."

"Yes," the Mantis said.

"There is much of which you must be advised," Chen said. "Other factors we must anticipate, if we are to share the fruits of your labor. Is it safe for you to listen?"

The Mantis looked around. The train was full, but he was alone in this small area, for the time being.

"Yes," he said.

"Ah, excellent," Master Chen replied. "Here is what the general has told me."

ABOUT FIVE MINUTES after Tai Pang had left, Han glanced up from the bench along the opposite wall.

"The Chinese word for railroad is *tielu*," Han said. "It means iron road. I imagine you have many trains such as this in your country, eh, Cooper-*jun*?" He had his shirt off and was undoing the straps for his artificial arm.

"We do," Bolan said. "Can't say I've had the chance to ride them much, though."

Han smiled as he pulled the prosthesis loose and rubbed his left stump. "It is much faster to fly. We have many air flights in China now."

Bolan nodded.

Han laughed. "You are too polite. Most people just come right out and ask me how I lost my arm."

Bolan said nothing.

"It was 1989. I was a young student, full of idealism," Han said. "We had assembled for a demonstration in Tiananmen Square. We thought it would usher in a new era of freedom in China. Mao Zedong was dead. His wife and the rest of her gang of four had been imprisoned. Our leader at the time, Deng Xiaoping, seemed to be a reasonable man who wanted to bring us back from the abyss of the Cultural Revolution."

Han closed his eyes and rocked his head back and forth, almost as if he were weeping. "One of my friends faced down a line of tanks that came to the square. We did not believe the soldiers would open fire on us, did not believe they would hurt their own people with such savagery. A bullet struck my left arm, up high, shattering the bone. It hung useless. I could not move." He sighed. "I was carried out of the area and just avoided being taken to prison, but the doctor who attended to me had very little formal training. He amputated my arm. My family managed to smuggle me out into the country, where they said the injury was the result of a farming accident."

"It sounds pretty bad," Bolan said.

"It was, but some change did come as a result. The Standing Committee made an unspoken agreement with the Chinese people." Han smiled wistfully. "Do not repeat the mistakes of Tiananmen Square, and we will grant you small freedoms, as we see fit."

"So in a way, you won. Your country's progressed."

Han shook his head, his face taking on a sad cast. "If you call what is happening now progress. We pollute our land, our rivers, our air, all in the name of advancing China. We steal land from the poor farmers, while corrupt politicians line their pockets. This is what I fight against—the humiliation of the poor, of the disenfranchised. I am their voice."

Bolan glanced at his watch again. It was closing in on twelve minutes since Tai Pang had left.

"There is a saying in my country," Han said. "When the Yellow River is at peace, China is at peace. They built the Sanmenxia Dam many years ago during Mao's Great Leap Forward. They said it would stop the floods that destroyed the farmland. Instead it made things much worse. Now heavy rains cause the reservoir to back up, and poisoned water rises over the banks. No one will acknowledge the mistake. Xie Chaoping was detained when he dared write about it."

"Is this political science lesson gonna go on much longer?" Grimaldi asked. "I would like to catch up on some sleep."

Han laughed. "I am sorry to wake you. My wife and granddaughter complain that I turn every dinner table discussion into a political lecture."

Bolan took out his satellite phone and checked the battery. It was dead, and he realized he hadn't charged it since before he'd arrived in Hong Kong. He slipped it back into his pocket and tapped Grimaldi's shoulder.

"I need your phone. Mine's dead."

Grimaldi made a series of grunts and groans as he turned over and retrieved the phone from the case on his belt. He glanced at it before handing it to Bolan. "Mine's starting to run low, too. Is there a place in here that we can charge them?"

"Different electrical current," Bolan said. "We'd need an adapter."

Herbie seemed to stir awake. "You want adapter, boss?" He stood up and stretched. "I get for you."

"Only if you can do it without attracting attention," Bolan said.

"Okay, boss. No sweat."

Yang had stirred awake, too. "I'll go with you."

Bolan shook his head. "Let Herbie go alone. It isn't wise for all of us to be seen together."

She shrugged and sat back down.

Herbie started for the door, but Bolan grabbed his arm. "See if you can find out what's keeping Tai Pang first."

"Yeah," Grimaldi said. "I'm getting hungry. Make sure he brings us some bottled water, too."

"Coming right up," Herbie said. He opened the door to the compartment, looked both ways, then slipped out.

Bolan checked to make sure no one else was in the hallway, then closed and locked the door. He turned back to Han.

"Tell me about the dragon key."

Han stared back at him, not answering.

"Mr. Han," Bolan said. "If we're going to get out of this safely, I need to know the whole story."

Han considered this, then nodded, waving for Bolan to step closer. Grimaldi cocked his head over the edge of the bunk.

"It is a memory stick," Han said. "It's concealed in a small plastic case that looks like the head of a dragon. Its owner wore it like a charm around his neck."

"Who's the owner?" Bolan asked.

Han was silent for a few more seconds, then said, "General Wong Su Tong of the People's Liberation Army."

Bolan and Grimaldi exchanged glances. The stakes had suddenly been raised.

"The dragon key, as he calls it, is purported to contain sensitive information of his corrupt activities."

"Purported?" Bolan asked.

"Yes. The general, for all his lasciviousness and greed, is a careful and intelligent man. He placed a cipher on the dragon key. I could not open it."

"A password?" Grimaldi said. "We've got people who could break that in a heartbeat. The Chinese honchos probably do, too, although it'd be a helluva lot simpler to just hold a gun to the general's johnson and force him to divulge it." He glanced down at Yang. "Sorry."

Yang smiled.

"Don't encourage him," Bolan said. "What exactly does the dragon key contain?"

"Secret Chinese and foreign bank accounts, as well

as the passwords for these accounts," Han said. "Transactions he has received for selling secrets of the Chinese military to foreign governments."

"Like Iran?" Bolan asked.

Han's eyebrows rose. "I see you know much more than I have told you, Cooper-*jun*."

"That's beside the point," Bolan said. "Does the general know you have it?"

A smile creased Han's face. "Let us say he knows it's missing, and has a strong suspicion that it's in my possession. The threat of exposure was what kept him from having me immediately arrested. I let it be known that if I were taken into custody, the dragon key would become public information." He looked at Bolan. "Now do you see why it is imperative that I go to Shanghai to recover it?"

"How did you find out about it?" Yang asked. "I mean, if I had something like that, I certainly wouldn't tell anyone."

"The general had a trusted aide," Han said. "One that was very adept at teaching him the ways of the computer. Long ago, her uncle was a student with me at the university. We were together at Tiananmen Square that day. Eventually she learned the extent of Wong's betrayal and confided in her uncle. He contacted me."

"A variation of the woman scorned, eh?" Grimaldi said.

"Where's the dragon key now?" Bolan asked.

Han smiled. "It is in Shanghai. In a very safe place."

"Mr. Han, I told you, we have to know it all."

"Not to mention that the three of us have been risking our lives to keep you safe, pal," Grimaldi said.

Han drew his mouth into a tight line, closed his eyes,

then nodded. "It's in a bank in Shanghai. In a safety deposit box."

"Does this box have a key?"

Han nodded, smiled and stuck his hand inside his artificial arm. After working his fingers around inside the prosthesis, he unpeeled a strip of duct tape and withdrew a thin metal key with a number stamped on the top.

Bolan nodded and told him to stow it again. "I'd better call in."

"And then some," Grimaldi said.

Bolan went to the door, opened it a crack and did a quick peek up and down the narrow aisle. "I'll be back."

"Give my regards to Hal," Grimaldi said.

Bolan slipped out. He exited the compartment and went in the opposite direction of the dining car. Bolan strolled to the end of the car and went into the gangway compartment. Accordion-like folds of rubber and canvas had been fastened around the gangway to interlock and seal off the compartment. Although it was noisy, Bolan figured it afforded him the privacy to make the quick call. He dialed the number for Brognola's phone and listened to several rings.

Finally, Hal answered. "What the hell, Jack? You know what time it is here?"

"Right greeting, wrong person," Bolan said.

"Why are you using Grimaldi's phone?"

"Mine's out of juice. We're running on fumes trying to get out of here. I wanted to call in a sitrep."

"Where are you at? A tin-can factory?"

"We're on a train." He gave Brognola a quick update on the situation, their itinerary and the dragon key.

Brognola gave a low whistle. "Okay, I'll brief the President and start greasing the wheels to get you guys out of there. Tressman, too. When you get where you're going, contact the American Consulate's office and we'll go from there."

"Sounds good," Bolan said. "I probably won't be able to check back with you. Jack's phone is about tapped out, too."

"Roger that, Striker," Brognola said. "Godspeed."

Bolan hung up. It was time to find Tai Pang.

10

The Mantis listened to Master Chen's final instructions carefully. The Triad boss ended with a stern admonishment.

"You must recover the dragon key at all costs," he said. "Do you understand?"

"Yes, Master," the Mantis replied.

"Let me hear you repeat this pledge."

"I will recover the dragon key." The Mantis suddenly became aware of the smell of a cigarette. He turned to see the one they called Herbie standing in the corner of the gangway compartment. The noise of the jolting train must have obscured the sound of the sliding door as he entered this section. Either that or he'd opened it surreptitiously. The Mantis ended his call abruptly and turned.

"Tai Pang, is that the food?" Herbie asked as he pointed to the paper sack on the floor. "The boss sent me to find you."

The Mantis felt like saying the big American was not his "boss," but instead he said nothing. He wondered just how much this cockroach had overheard. At least they were alone in this small area.

Herbie inhaled his cigarette and blew out a cloudy

breath as he talked. "Master, huh? Who were you talking to? And what's the dragon key?"

The Mantis stared at him without speaking.

"Hey, listen." Herbie held up his hands. "I have no problem if you have another angle to play. In fact, I'll help you with it. Just let me get my money from the Americans first, okay?"

The Mantis considered his options.

Herbie puffed nervously on the cigarette. The ash glowed with a sudden brightness, and he exhaled smoke through both nostrils. "I know how it is. We're cut from the same cloth. I grew up poor, too, but that doesn't mean I intend to stay that way. You and me, we're the same, right?"

Again, the Mantis said nothing, but he felt rage building within him. *The same?* How could this insect have the audacity to speak those words?

Suddenly, the door to the main compartment slid open and a uniformed train conductor stepped into the area adjacent to the gangway. He looked at them, nodded in an officious sort of way and asked, "Is there a problem here?"

Herbie flashed a nervous smile. He held up his cigarette, which was now burned down to the end, and said, "Hey, friend, do you have any smokes? I can pay."

The conductor's right eyebrow elevated slightly. After a second's pause, he nodded and took out a large ring of keys. "In my locker," he said as he went to the luggage compartment, unlocked the door and opened it. Inside he slipped another key into the lock of a thin metal closet. He twisted the key and pulled the door open, revealing a locker approximately thirty centimeters wide and at least fifty deep. The Mantis could see a dressy jacket hanging inside. The conductor fumbled with a package of cigarettes on the top shelf.

As the man turned back to them, the Mantis pivoted. A hooking kick hit the conductor in the abdomen. As he bent over, grasping his gut, the ring of keys clattered on the metal floor. The Mantis stepped in with a ridge hand blow that swept upward, striking the man's throat. He reeled, gasping, as the Mantis encircled the conductor's neck with a guillotine choke and punctuated the movement with a sharp twisting motion.

Herbie heard the neck snap.

Instead of letting the conductor slump completely to the floor, the Mantis held him and began stripping off his uniform shirt.

"What did you do that for?" Herbie asked.

The Mantis could smell the cockroach's sweat. "Take that jacket out of the locker," he said.

Herbie stood frozen for a moment, and the Mantis flashed an angry stare that got the insect going with herky-jerky movements. The Mantis glanced in both directions as he stripped off the uniform shirt and told Herbie to slip the jacket from the locker over the dead man's arms. So far, they were still alone. When they had tugged the jacket over the arms and shoulders of the corpse, the Mantis shoved the man into the luggage van, lowering him to a sitting position. Reaching into his pocket, the Mantis wrapped his fingers around the British agent's gun. He hated to use such a shiny souvenir, but it was necessary. The ruse must continue until he had the dragon key.

"What do you want me to do now?" Herbie asked.

"I want you to join him," the Mantis said.

The cockroach looked down, then back up, grinning with that same nervous expression.

The Mantis removed the Walther from his pocket, shoved it against Herbie's belly and pulled the trigger twice. It was as the Mantis had hoped. The popping sound of the gun was muffled by their close proximity and the jolting squeal of the train.

Herbie stiffened with each shot, his eyes wide with horror.

The Mantis stepped closer, knowing the other man had but a few seconds of life left.

"Remember this as you die, insect," the Mantis said, their faces millimeters apart, "we are *not* the same."

BOLAN CAUGHT SIGHT of Tai Pang running down the aisle toward their compartment. As soon as their eyes locked, the man motioned for Bolan to come with him, and he turned and ran in the opposite direction.

This doesn't look good, Bolan thought as he trotted after the lithe figure.

Bolan followed him into the gangway compartment. A second later Tai Pang glanced both ways, then stopped. A man and a woman walked through the gangway connection and into the next car. Tai Pang waited until they'd gone and pulled out a ring of keys, opening the sliding door to the luggage compartment. Two men sat on the floor, slumped against the rows of suitcases. One of them was Herbie. Both were obviously dead.

"What happened?" Bolan asked. He smelled the residual odor of burned gunpowder and saw two expended shell casings vibrating on the metal floor with the train's movement. They appeared to be .380 rounds.

"That man shot Herbie," Tai Pang said, pulling a small, stainless-steel pistol partially out of his pocket. "He was secret police. They must know we're on the train. I had to kill him."

Bolan glanced around. So far, they were still alone.

"We must dump their bodies off the train," Tai Pang said. "Before they are discovered."

"These doors are probably autolocked," Bolan said. "They're designed not to open while the train's in motion."

Tai Pang held up the ring of keys and pointed to a square box on the wall. "That's the manual override to unlock the door." He stepped forward and stuck a key into the slot and the box opened. Bolan wondered how Tai Pang knew about the override box, and also something else...

"Where'd you get those keys?" Bolan asked.

"I stole them," Tai Pang said. "From a conductor."

"And how did you know about the override box?"

"My father worked for the railroad." Tai Pang gestured toward the cop. "I'll get that one." He grabbed the dead man, dragged him over to the door and pressed a switch. The door popped open slightly and a cold rush of air whistled in. Bolan dragged Herbie's body over to the door. He reached down and closed Herbie's eyes. It wasn't much of a send-off, but it was all he could do.

Tai Pang gripped the handle on the big sliding door and pulled it all the way open. The dark night rushed past. Bolan could see little else besides a smattering of gravel and flashes of periodic, adjacent metal structures. Tai Pang positioned himself by the open space and tossed Herbie's body out first. Bolan noticed the two blackened holes, surrounded by splotches of crimson, on the dead man's gut.

Powder burns on his shirt, Bolan thought. A close-range shot. Very close.

Tai Pang grabbed the other man and threw him out, as well. Bolan didn't see any obvious wounds on that

guy, but from the way the dead man's head loosely bobbled, his neck appeared broken.

Standing, Tai Pang took the pistol out of his pocket
and looked at it.

A Walther PPS, Bolan thought. Stainless steel. An
expensive weapon for a plainclothes cop.

Tai Pang drew his arm back to toss the gun out, but
Bolan said, "Hey, maybe we'd better keep that. We may
need all the firepower we can get."

Tai Pang nodded and slipped the gun back into his
pocket.

Bolan shoved the door closed. "Let's get back to the
compartment and sort this out."

"Okay." Tai Pang bent and grabbed a large paper bag
that was on the floor. "The food," he said, holding the
bag up. There were traces of blood on his hands, which
had stained the paper with red smudges.

Bolan nodded and pulled back the door to the interior of the car.

They saw no one on their way back to the compartment. Bolan opened the door and they slipped inside.

"Ah, fried rice and egg rolls," Grimaldi said, rub-
bing his hands together. "My favorite."

"Herbie's dead," Bolan said.

"What?" Yang's face crinkled in horror.

Han's brow furrowed. "How did this happen?"

Tai Pang looked at Bolan, said nothing.

"Apparently, he was accosted by a plainclothes po-
liceman," Bolan said. "There must have been some kind
of struggle and Herbie was shot at close range. The other
man's dead, too."

"Oh, how terrible." Yang wiped some tears from her
eyes.

"Well, I guess we won't be buying him that new

van after all." Grimaldi shrugged. "I'll kind of miss the little guy."

Bolan gestured for Tai Pang to place the bag of food on the bench. "Watch out, there's blood on the outside of the bag." He looked down and saw tiny splattering along the top fold, as well as the smudges Tai Pang's bloody fingers had left. Bolan took out his Espada and cut the bag down each side, exposing the cartons of food and six bottles of water.

"I don't think I want to eat right now," Yang said.

"You've got no choice." Bolan handed her one of the cartons and some chopsticks. "It's only a matter of time before they discover we're on this train. They probably already searched the one going to Hong Kong." He handed a box of rice to Han, and one to Grimaldi.

Grimaldi popped his open and started shoveling the contents into his mouth.

Bolan held a box toward Tai Pang, who shook his head and said he needed to wash his hands. He went into the small washroom and closed the door behind him.

"So what's our contingency plan?" Grimaldi asked.

Bolan opened a box and began eating. "Good question. It's going to depend on how far we get before they stop this train and search it." He turned to Han. "You know your country better than we do. Any suggestions?"

Han chewed slowly on some rice before answering, "I would say we are still perhaps six or seven hundred kilometers from Shanghai. That is a sizable distance."

"I have an idea," Tai Pang said as he exited the washroom.

They looked at him.

"This is the high-speed line used by the bullet trains and the sleepers," he said. "There is a freight train route that runs parallel to these tracks. It is a few kilometers to the west."

"What's the terrain like between these tracks and the freight line?" Bolan asked.

"Farmland. Rice paddies," Tai Pang said. "We can walk."

Bolan mulled over the plan. They'd be trying to move on foot, in the dark, with no compass and the possibility of armed PLA soldiers in pursuit. Then they'd wait for a southbound freight moving slow enough to board. Plus, there was the little matter of jumping off this train, which was moving at a pretty good clip. But if the authorities did eventually stop this train, there weren't a lot of options.

"Do you know how often those freight trains run?" Bolan asked.

Tai Pang shook his head. "I do not."

"Well, let's keep it in mind," Bolan said. "Hopefully, we'll be able to get a lot closer to Shanghai before we have to jump ship. But if this train stops, be ready."

He looked at each of them, noticing their grim expressions as they ate in silence. Something else gnawed at Bolan, but he couldn't grasp it through the fatigue.

GENERAL WONG SAT in his office and stared at his personal cell phone. After the discovery of the Hong Kong bullet train ruse, he'd had little choice but to implement the stop-and-search order for all trains that had left Beijing in the past twelve hours. To do less would create more suspicion in the Standing Committee.

They had already expressed their displeasure with the way the matter had been handled. And the news about the missing guidance system had been discovered as well, furthering the Committee's ire. Someone was going to pay dearly.

Wong knew his best—his only—chance to avoid discovery was to remain in command of the investigation and make a good show of trying to capture Han and the Americans. Naturally, he would see to it they all perished in an "attempted resistance," but he also had to recover the dragon key first.

If Han did have a plan in place to deliver the dragon key to the journalists, and if they could somehow crack his password, the result would be immediate and deadly for him. But if Wong could get his hands on Han, there were ways of making him talk. He would keep the man alive just long enough to get the location of the dragon key.

Wong looked at the phone again, willing it to ring. Where was the update from that bastard Chen?

The phone rang. He grabbed it, glanced at the number and answered.

"Things are proceeding well." Chen's calm voice did little to soothe Wong's anxiety.

"You have found it?"

"Not yet. But we are getting closer. How is your train search proceeding?"

Wong snorted. "I delayed things as long as I could with that Hong Kong train, but they would get suspicious if I did not enact more sweeping actions. I cannot appear as a total fool in their eyes."

Chen chuckled. "A wise man is often thought of as a fool until the light shines upon his wisdom."

More Confucian nonsense. Wong was in no mood for it. "My soldiers will be stopping the Shanghai sleeper train in Jiangsu Province shortly. Are your people in place?"

"They are," Chen said. "When Han and the Americans abandon the train, Lee will take them to the freight lines, ostensibly to complete their journey to Shanghai. My men will be waiting for them. But I still feel it would be better to wait until they have retrieved the dragon key in Shanghai."

"And take the chance of losing them again?" Wong said.

"Lee will not let that happen. And we still do not know its exact location. Remember, the smart fox follows the rabbit back to his lair in order to feast on a larger bounty."

Wong started to swear, but stopped. He could not afford to lose his temper with this son of a whore. Not at this time. Not while he held all the pieces of the puzzle.

"Regardless," Chen said, "You should begin your journey south, to Shanghai, so we'll be able to ascertain the validity of the dragon key once it is recovered."

"I have a plane standing by," Wong said. "Call me back when you have them."

And with that, he hung up. It was time for him to begin his exit strategy to leave China forever. All he needed was that elusive dragon key.

11

Bolan was woken by the jolt of the train suddenly slowing down. He wasn't sure how long he'd been under. At Grimaldi's insistence, he'd agreed to take a nap and had fallen asleep almost immediately.

"I think the engineer just hit the brakes," Grimaldi said.

Bolan looked out the window. It was still dark. He checked his watch: 2149. An hour and a half since he'd lain down. The train had probably traveled another hundred or so kilometers. They were still a good distance from Shanghai.

He swung off the bunk and jumped to the floor. Han and Yang were both on their feet. Grimaldi was at the door holding his SIG Sauer.

"Where's Tai Pang?" Bolan asked, grabbing his Beretta as he slipped into his shoulder holster.

"I sent him to try to find out what's going on." Grimaldi peeked out the partially open door. "He's coming back now."

Grimaldi opened the door and Tai Pang slid through the opening.

"The PLA has set up a blockade," he said. "Apparently, they're stopping and searching all trains departing Beijing."

The jig's up, Bolan thought. He'd anticipated this move. Now the process of elimination had caught up to them. Once the train came to a complete stop, the soldiers would do a car-by-car search.

"Come on," Bolan said. "We're going to have to jump off now."

"Before we've stopped?" Han asked.

"Before we're surrounded," Bolan said.

Bolan and Grimaldi grabbed their bags and moved to the door. Tai Pang and Yang went first, followed by Han and then the two Americans. They started down the corridor toward the exit when a uniformed conductor appeared holding his palms up. He said something in Mandarin, which Bolan took to be an admonishment to return to their compartment. Tai Pang lashed out with a blur of punches and the conductor collapsed to the floor.

"Looks like that guy got his ticket punched," Grimaldi said.

"We've got to keep moving," Bolan said.

"I will put him in our compartment," Tai Pang said. "You go to the door of the train."

Bolan motioned the others to go, stepped back to the compartment and held the door open. Tai Pang dragged the conductor inside and reached into his pocket, the *balisong* suddenly opening in his hand with a flash as he grabbed the unconscious conductor's hair.

"Don't kill him," Bolan said.

Tai Pang hesitated. "He will identify us. They'll know we were on this train."

"They'll figure that out either way," Bolan said. "He's just a man doing his job. He doesn't deserve to die."

Tai Pang held the knife above the conductor's throat, his eyes fixing Bolan with a cold stare. He dropped the man's head, stood and flipped the knife closed. "Very well. Let's go."

"That looks like a Filipino knife," Bolan said as Tai Pang dropped it into his pocket. "A *balisong*."

Tai Pang shot him a hard stare. "You are correct. I like shiny things."

"Those Filipinos know how to handle knives," Bolan said.

"As do I."

Bolan pressed the button to lock the compartment door from the inside and slammed it shut. He and Tai Pang hurried down the corridor and met the others in the small anteroom by the exit doors.

The scenery was still rushing by the glass window of the door, but at a much slower rate. Bolan estimated that the train was traveling about twenty-five to thirty miles per hour. The ground next to the tracks was a hill of gravel. It would be a rough landing.

Tai Pang took out the keys and unlocked the override box, then pressed the switch. The door popped open slightly, and Bolan pulled it all the way back and glanced out. The adjacent grade appeared to be free of any structural dangers, like telephone or electric poles. It was just a long, hard, stony slope. Farther down the tracks, he could see an array of vehicles and the glimmer of several sets of headlights perhaps half a mile away. They had to go now or they'd be seen, for sure.

"I'll go first," he said. "Follow me in rapid succession." He motioned to Grimaldi to jump last. "Curl your body up into a ball and try to relax as you land."

With that admonishment, Bolan stepped through the opening. He felt himself sail through the darkness for about two and a half seconds before his feet hit the uneven gravelly surface with a punishing jolt. It was like landing in a drop zone after a parachute jump. Bolan rolled with the impact, lessening the severity, and got to his feet in time to see the next figure sailing through the darkness. It was Yang. He paused to help her up and saw Han, his good arm extended and holding his prosthesis, flying toward the ground. He landed hard and rolled. Bolan knelt next to him and saw that he was unconscious, his artificial arm nowhere to be seen.

Tai Pang jumped next, landing with the gracefulness of a jungle cat, and then Grimaldi with his suitcase in hand. His landing was somewhat less than perfect.

Bolan lifted Han onto his shoulder and trotted toward Grimaldi, who was getting up slower than normal.

"You all right?" Bolan asked.

"Ah, twisted my ankle," Grimaldi said. "But I'm good to go. How's Sammo?"

"Down for the count. Plus, his arm's missing." Bolan scanned the area. "You got your night-vision goggles handy?"

"I have the arm," Tai Pang said. He held it up.

"I'll take it."

Tai Pang looked at him momentarily, then handed the prosthesis to the Executioner.

"Let's see what star light, star bright tells us." Grimaldi unzipped his bag and pulled out his night-vision goggles. "Don't leave home without them."

Bolan grinned. "That fancy suitcase is going to make one of these rice farmers a nice pig trough."

"In your dreams," Grimaldi said, looking through the binocular function of the goggles. "Looks like farmland leading up to a built-up area. Lots of high-rise buildings in the distance."

"Good," Bolan said. "Maybe we can find a car somewhere. Which way is best?"

"There's a path straight ahead."

Yang and Tai Pang joined them and they all began a quick trot into the dark, expansive field. Soon they came to a barbed-wire fence. Han had stirred awake during the trek and said he was able to walk. Bolan set him down and gave him his arm back. He held it tightly to his chest. Grimaldi was showing the others how to go underneath the fence in a supine position. Bolan and Han followed.

On the other side, three-foot mud walls housed row after row of budding plants springing up out of a layer of water. Grimaldi led the way along one of the walls that bisected the entire field. Yang and Tai Pang followed him with Han and Bolan bringing up the rear.

Han was obviously having trouble balancing on the top of the barrier and slowed considerably.

"I do not think I can continue," he said. "Save yourselves. Go on without me."

Bolan glanced back and saw the lit train stopped about half a mile from where they'd jumped off. The search had undoubtedly begun. "Not an option. I'll carry you." Bolan shouldered the smaller man once again and began a quick trot to catch up to the others.

Finally they reached a solid patch of ground that led to an old wooden house. A ramshackle barn lay about a hundred feet to the left, with a corral and a plow sitting in front of it. A huge ox stood slumbering inside the fenced-in area. Bolan paused and lowered Han to the ground. He took a few deep breaths and held up his prosthesis. "At least I was able to hold on to my arm."

"Anybody want to try to play cowboy?" Grimaldi asked, pointing to the ox.

"Let's check the barn," Bolan said. "Maybe he has a truck."

"That is doubtful," Han said. "He's so poor, he plows the field with an ox. I don't think he'd even have a telephone. This is another example of the division between the rich and corrupt and the poor."

"We must hurry," Tai Pang said. "The soldiers will be coming after us, and the other railroad tracks are still five or six kilometers from here."

"You know," Grimaldi said as he continued to look through the night-vision goggles. "It looks like there's a built-up area over there about one klick away." He pointed to the southwest.

"Let's go for it," Bolan said.

"But we'll lose time," Tai Pang insisted. "We should keep moving to the west, through the paddies."

Bolan shook his head. "We go this way."

They angled southwest through another set of rice paddies, replete with the mud barriers that served as walking paths. Bolan continued to glance back in the direction of the train. It looked like a small lit-up toy now.

The rice paddy gave way to a barren field, pockmarked with numerous ditches and large holes. Grimaldi led them through the erratic ground until they came to a street, across from which a series of modern-looking high-rises sprung up lighted only by moonlight.

"No lights anywhere," Grimaldi said. "Everybody's asleep."

"Not sleeping," Han said. "It is an abandoned city. We are in Jiangsu Province."

"Abandoned?" Grimaldi said. "Why'd all the people leave?"

Han gestured with his good arm. "They were never here, except for the farmers, who were forced out. This is one more example of the corruption that rules China today. The politicians in this province took the land from the farmers and sold it to developers at a cheap price, who then built these buildings in anticipation of new housing that was never needed. The politicians were bribed to force the farmers to sell, and then the farmers were never paid." He looked down and shook his head sadly. "Do you see how corruption has polluted not only our air and water, but the good earth itself?"

"The Good Earth," Grimaldi said. "Pearl Buck, right? I read that book in school."

Han's smile was sad.

"Keep moving," Bolan said. "Let's see if we can find a place to hunker down and get our bearings."

"Looks like we can take our pick," Grimaldi said, then stopped. "Hey, wait."

Bolan heard it, too: the sound of an engine cycling in the darkness.

"I thought you said this area was abandoned."

"It is," Han said.

"Well, somebody's here," Grimaldi said. "Squatters, maybe?"

"Let's take a look," Bolan said. "Yang, stay here with Sammo. The rest of us will check things out."

Tai Pang seemed to stiffen at Bolan issuing orders, but he moved forward. Bolan and Grimaldi readied their weapons as they moved quickly across the dark, empty street and on to the next one. The sputtering got louder. They flattened against the wall of a building and Grimaldi used his night-vision goggles.

"A generator over there," he whispered. "And a truck and motorcycle."

Bolan turned to Tai Pang. "Who do you think they are?"

He studied the scene, then said, "They are thieves.

They steal the metals from these buildings and sell it on the black market."

"See any guards?" Bolan asked.

Grimaldi peered through the night-vision goggles again. "Uh-uh. Lights flashing on the first floor, though."

"Let's get closer," Bolan said, and moved across the street.

When he got to the truck, he paused by the cab and slowly opened the door. No keys in the ignition but a bundle of wires hung down from under the dashboard. He motioned for Grimaldi to check it out.

"Think you can hot-wire this thing?" Bolan asked.

"Does a bear shit in the woods?" Grimaldi said with a grin. "Got a knife?"

Bolan gave him the Espada and moved along the bed of the truck. The motorcycle was parked about ten feet away. No keys in that one, either. If they couldn't hot-wire it, they'd have to disable it or risk the chance of pursuit by the scavengers.

The truck's engine turned over once, sputtered out. Cycled again, and caught.

Bolan watched the entrance of the building to see if the noise from the generator had covered the sound of the truck starting up. Grimaldi flashed a thumbs-up and got down next to Bolan. Voices emanated from inside the building and two men rushed out, one holding a long pipe wrench, the other a hammer.

Tai Pang jumped forward and delivered a thrusting side kick to the guy with the hammer. As he folded and collapsed, the one with the wrench swung it in a looping arc. Tai Pang ducked under the swing, spinning so that his extended leg swept the wrench-wielder's feet out from under him. The guy fell onto his back. Tai Pang leaped into the air and came down on the man's throat, twisting his leg with a lethal punctuation. The first guy was getting to his feet, the hammer dangling from his hand. Tai Pang spun toward him, catching the juncture of neck and body with a spinning kick that looked as though it broke the guy's neck. His head bobbled loosely as he fell forward.

Something shiny clattered to the sidewalk as Tai Pang landed. It was the Walther PPS.

Two more men rushed out of the building, each holding long metal rods. Tai Pang leaped toward them, jolting one with two snapping front kicks: one to the right knee, the second to the face. The man stumbled, and Tai Pang ripped the metal rod out of his hands. He whirled, using the bar to block a blow by the second assailant. The metal bar flashed upward, knocking the bar from the second man's grasp. The hard metallic end drove into the throat of the first assailant, then across the neck of the second.

"Damn, he's pretty good at that, isn't he?" Grimaldi said.

"A little too good sometimes."

They rushed forward as a fifth man peered out from inside the building. He took one look at his fallen compatriots and started to run back inside. Tai Pang adjusted his grip on the metal rod, cocked his arm back and threw it like a javelin. It sailed straight into the back of the running man.

Bolan stooped and picked up the Walther Tai Pang had dropped as the redoubtable fighter ran toward the last of the scavengers. Tai Pang jumped high in the air and landed feetfirst on the prone body of the last man.

Something caught Bolan's eye. The Walther had a stainless-steel sheen, with *TNT* engraved on the slide in fancy script. *TNT*... Thomas Norris Trent, the murdered MI6 agent. There was only one way Tai Pang could have gotten this gun.

Bolan looked up, and in that moment locked eyes with Tai Pang. A silent realization seemed to pass between them.

Bolan raised his Beretta, about to fire a round, when Tai Pang turned and ran deeper into the building, slipping around a corner and disappearing into the darkness.

"What the hell?" Grimaldi said. "I thought he was on our side."

"So did I, until now," Bolan said. "He's Triad."

"Damn. Well, let's go track him down, then. I don't want a dude like him on our tail."

Bolan shook his head. "No time. Let's check these guys for keys and get out of here. Remember we've still got the PLA breathing down our necks."

Grimaldi grunted, knelt by the first dead scavenger and started going through the man's pockets. He found keys to the truck and the motorcycle on the second man.

"Take his wallet," Bolan said. "Let's see if he's got a Chinese driver's license Han can use in case we get stopped."

Grimaldi checked the man's rear pants pocket and pulled out a thick wallet. "Well, if we do get stopped we still have enough yuan to bribe our way out of it. We're taking the truck, I assume?"

"And the bike," Bolan said. "We can use those long boards as a ramp to push it up into the back."

"Damn, a sport bike," Grimaldi said with a grin. "I hope none of my Harley buddies find out about this."

THEY LEFT THE bodies lying where they'd fallen and drove off in the truck. Bolan found a loose-fitting hat,

which he jammed on his head to obscure his features
as much as he could. The height of the truck aided in
that subterfuge. He figured by canting his head slightly
each time a vehicle came along side of them, the wide
brim of the hat would do the trick. It was still dark as
well, which would help.

Han sat beside him in the cab, with Yang and
Grimaldi out of sight in the back with the motorcycle
and rolls of stolen copper wire. A small sliding window
behind the seat of the truck opened into the truck's bed.

Han directed him to a modern superhighway, and
he accelerated to a speed just over the limit. He hoped
that cops in China gave speeders the same customary
modified grace as coppers in the States did. Soon they
were joined by other vehicles all traveling southbound
toward Shanghai.

"How much farther do you think it is?" Bolan asked.

Han looked around. "Perhaps four or five hundred
kilometers to Shanghai. Then we will have to negoti-
ate the city. It is a magnificent metropolis. Much like
your city of New York, I am told."

Bolan glanced at his watch: 0330. They had maybe
five or six hours of driving ahead of them, barring any
unforeseen stops or detours. The gas gauge showed full
for now. They'd been lucky in that respect. And Tai
Pang was probably left floundering in the abandoned
city, trying to dodge the PLA. That might buy them
some extra time.

Han heaved a sigh and looked at Bolan. "I have not
thanked you for saving my life back there."

"Thank me when I get you safely to the American
Consulate," Bolan said. "Besides, I didn't do much."

Han laughed. "You rescued me from the Triad killers at my house, and then you carried me when I had

no strength to go on. You, and your two friends, continue to risk your lives on my behalf."

Bolan said nothing.

Han continued. "When I was a youth, I used to watch the pirated movies from Hong Kong. They depicted wonderful Chinese heroes. Role models for Chinese youth. We needed those heroes. We still do."

"Everybody needs a good hero," Bolan said.

Han laughed. "My favorite actor was Jimmy Wang Yu. He played a character called the One-Armed Swordsman in several movies. Have you ever seen them?"

"I don't watch too many movies."

"No, you live them." Han sighed. "When I was young, I used to dream that I could be like him one day." He laughed bitterly. "And now I have come to this."

Bolan searched for something to say, but found nothing.

The small window behind them slid open, and Grimaldi's face appeared.

"You know, a little heat back here would be nice," he said. "Not that we're complaining or anything."

"Mr. Han estimates we'll be there in about five or six hours," Bolan said. "With a little luck on our side."

"Damn," Grimaldi said. "And I left my four-leaf clover back in the States."

"Four-leaf clover?" Han asked.

"A good luck piece," Bolan said.

Han nodded. "I understand. Do you like to gamble, Mr. Grimaldi?"

"Only on a sure thing."

"A sure thing?" Han's brow wrinkled. "I do not understand your words."

"It's an idiom," Bolan said. He turned slightly and glanced at Grimaldi. "Now say good-night, Jack."

"Good-night, Jack," Grimaldi said. "Wake us when we get there."

He slammed the window shut.

If we get there, Bolan thought.

THEY RODE IN silence for long stretches, stopping for gas twice at isolated stations. Bolan kept his head down and pumped the fuel while Han, his artificial arm in his pocket, passed a handful of yuan to the attendant. Finally, they neared the outskirts of the huge city. The rising sun was shining over the roadway and more and more cars began to appear. Han perked up and directed Bolan to take the North-South Elevated Roadway. It fanned out into six lanes, each full of speeding vehicles. The skyline looked massive, modern and endless.

"What's the best way to get to the office of the American Consulate?" Bolan asked.

Han told him to keep going straight. "It's near Boai Hospital. That is where I got my new arm." He patted the prosthesis. "The Shanghai Library is close, as well."

"I'll have to check that out on my next trip." Bolan reached back and banged on the window. After a few moments it slid open and Grimaldi's face appeared again.

"Can't a guy get any sleep around here?" he said with a grin.

"Sleep when this is over," Bolan said. "We're getting close to the consulate."

They were almost over the hump, but they still had the police and the PLA on their tail, and they were fighting the clock.

"Let's go directly to the American Consulate's office and take refuge there. We can check on the status of your family and arrange for you to get political asylum in the United States."

Han said nothing.

"Yeah," Grimaldi said. "If you like Shanghai, you're gonna love Las Vegas."

"Cooper-*jun*," Han said. "By all means, you and your friends go to the Consulate. But as I told you, I cannot leave China without first picking up the dragon key."

Bolan frowned. This man was as stubborn as a country mule.

"Okay, where's this bank at?" he asked.

Han gave him an address.

Bolan smiled as the roadway expanded to ten lanes. "Maybe we'll call a taxi. I'm getting a little tired of fighting all this traffic."

THEIR DRIVE PAST the office of the American Consulate on Haui Hai Zhang Road revealed two things: the place looked like an antebellum mansion, except that there were at least three plainclothes police strolling around the driveway entrance. The huge house was set far back from the street with an expansive green lawn in between. The American flag flew proudly from a flagpole in front, and Bolan thought how welcome the sight of the Stars and Stripes was. He downshifted and kept going.

"Looks like they've got a welcoming committee set up in front of the place," Bolan said.

"Can we crash through with the truck?" Grimaldi asked.

"That would not be advisable," Han said.

"Mr. Han, he's joking."

"I am?" Grimaldi said.

Bolan turned right at the next corner and said, "Give me your SIG."

"I beg your pardon?" Grimaldi said. "Git yer own gun."

Bolan held up his hand and Grimaldi heaved an exaggerated sigh and smacked the SIG Sauer into Bolan's palm.

"Mags, too," Bolan said.

"Damn, why don't you take shoes and socks while you're at it?" Grimaldi handed over two full magazines. "Or maybe my underwear, since I already feel naked."

Yang's face appeared beside Grimaldi. "Speaking of feeling naked, my cell phone battery's dead."

Grimaldi sighed. "The story of my life."

Bolan pulled to a stop at the curb, shifted to Neutral and yanked the hand brake. "You can charge it up inside the consulate. Jack, let's get the motorcycle out. You and Yang use it to zoom past those coppers and get inside the gate while I create a distraction. Once you're in there, identify yourselves as Americans and let them know we're going to need emergency assistance. Mr. Han and I will follow once we get the dragon key." He reached in his pocket and pulled out his satellite phone. "Here, get this charged up, too."

"Great plan," Yang said, "but I'm sticking with you two."

Bolan turned to look at her. Her pretty face was framed in the window with a serious expression drawn across it. "We don't have time to debate the issue."

"You're right," she said. "We don't. So accept the fact that I'm going with you and Sammo."

"But—"

"No buts, Mr. Cooper. You don't speak Mandarin.

You can't even listen to what's being said around you. Face it, you need me."

Bolan took a deep breath and noticed Han sitting there with a wide grin on his face.

"It seems that American women are very much the same as Chinese," he said. "Always the secret boss."

Bolan thought about it. With Grimaldi inside greasing the wheels for their safe passage out of the country, maybe it would be prudent to let Yang join them. She did speak the language and could easily fade into the crowd and get back to the consulate if something went wrong.

"Give Hal a sitrep when you get inside," Bolan said to Grimaldi.

"What about me?" Yang asked.

"We'll stop at an electronics store on the way to the bank and get you a new battery," he said. "So you'll feel fully clothed."

She smiled and nodded.

BOLAN TOOK ANOTHER spin around the block, this time accelerating loudly and grinding the gears to attract attention as Grimaldi rode alongside the truck on the motorcycle. Bolan barreled past the front gate, diverting the attention of the three men he assumed to be police, while Grimaldi made a quick right turn into the gate area, zooming around the barrier and heading down the long drive toward the huge white mansion.

Hopefully, he won't give the guards too hard a time, Bolan thought.

He concentrated on driving, brushing off the lingering fatigue. It was 0923. He estimated that he'd slept a total of four hours in the past forty-eight.

Traffic was so heavy on Huaihai Middle Road that

Yang was able to jump out at an electronics store and buy a new, fully charged battery for her cell phone. When she climbed into the truck cab next to Han, Bolan told her to call the consulate to check on Grimaldi. After spending a good five minutes on hold, she was finally able to ascertain that "an unidentified man, claiming to be an American, was indeed inside and was being interviewed at this time."

"That means he's running the show," Bolan said with a grin. He glanced in both mirrors. Traffic was almost at a standstill. "How close are we to the bank, Mr. Han?"

"I'm afraid it is some distance," Han said. "It's in the Pu Dong District."

"We could take the subway," Yang said. "It's right up there."

"What about this truck?" Han asked.

Bolan veered toward an intersection. "It's time to dump this thing anyway."

After leaving the truck in an alleyway, they began a swift walk toward the subway. On the way they stopped at a small restaurant and bought bottles of water and some greasy meat and gravy poured over a slice of bread.

The subway proved much faster and less noticeable than the truck as it whisked them underneath the bustling city streets and the Huang Pu River, as well. As they emerged from the underground system Bolan told both of them to stay on the penultimate landing while he did some reconnoitering. The streets were busy with a flood of endless vehicular and pedestrian traffic. He spied an empty taxi and waved. The driver pulled to the curb and Bolan motioned for Yang and Han to join him. They hopped inside the cab and Han gave the address to the driver. He eyed them warily until Bolan slipped a large amount of currency over the seat. The driver's eyes widened and he grinned.

"Tell him to wait for us outside the bank," Bolan said.

Yang relayed the message and the driver nodded.

As the taxi weaved in and out of the heavy traffic, Bolan thought about their next steps. Get to the bank, get the dragon key, then make their way back to the consulate. The subway might be their best bet, but he'd have the cab drop them someplace close, but not obvious.

When they finally got to the bank, Han instructed the driver to pull over about fifty feet from the front entrance. He turned to Bolan.

"Cooper-*jun,* may I suggest you wait here?"

Bolan considered this. "It would be safer for me to go with you."

Han laughed. "That would also attract much attention. You are a very large man."

"I'll go with you," Yang said. "Nobody will look twice at the two of us."

Bolan took a deep breath and glanced out the windows at the constant stream of humanity. They'd taken pains to vary their approach here, so he doubted anyone could have followed them, plus, how would anyone know about this particular bank?

"Mr. Han, you're sure no one else knows about this location?"

Han shook his head. "No one. I did not even tell my family for fear it would put them in danger."

Bolan nodded. "Try to make it quick."

He watched as Han, wearing his artificial arm, and Yang got out of the cab and walked leisurely down the street.

They were right, he thought. They looked like two ordinary Chinese citizens strolling down the sidewalk.

A big American tagging along would attract too much attention. They both went inside the bank.

I just hope they're fast, he thought.

As Bolan scanned the other end of the block, the driver suddenly exclaimed, "Hey, American! Look! Your friends got trouble." The cab driver pointed through the window.

Three men were pushing Yang and Mr. Han into a black van. One of them was Tai Pang.

How the hell did he find us? Bolan thought as he whipped out his Beretta and started to open the door of the taxi. Tai Pang jumped into the van and it took off. The two other men got into a second van and that one slipped into traffic, as well.

"You speak English?" Bolan asked.

"I got English, little bit," the driver said.

Bolan reached into his pocket and pulled out a fist full of yuan. "Follow that first van. The one with my friends."

The driver's eyes widened. He twisted in his seat and jammed the taxi into gear, barely looking as he zoomed into traffic to the accompaniment of several sets of squealing brakes and honking horns behind them.

"No worry," the driver said. "I catch 'em."

12

The van bounced as it pulled off the street and onto the mud-and-gravel road that led to the construction area beside the river. The Mantis waited for the van to come to a complete stop before he opened the door and hopped out. He told his men to wait before taking the prisoners out of the vehicle, and then he ran back to the second van, which was pulling onto the road, as well.

"Park down there," the Mantis said, pointing to a series of broken-down buildings that stood in sharp contrast to the spiraling skyscrapers just beyond the roadway. "Stay here and make sure no one follows."

The driver grunted in agreement.

The Mantis walked back to the first van, got in and motioned for the driver to continue.

"Why are you doing this?" Yang asked in English.

He regarded her coldly and replied in Mandarin, "You would do well to beg for mercy in my native language. You are, after all, in my country."

"Please," Han said, "let her go. You have me. She is not part of this."

The Mantis turned, and his arm shot over the front seat, slapping Han across the mouth. "Traitor, shut your mouth."

"You call *me* a traitor?" Han said, blood coating his

front teeth. "You are the one who seeks to betray his own people for money."

The Mantis thought about punching him again, but he knew the master had forbidden it. He wanted Han delivered intact.

A man holding a shotgun appeared at the corner of a building and pointed to his left. The van slowed to a stop and the driver rotated the wheel, pulling behind a three-sided structure that hid the vehicle from the roadway above. Two other vehicles were already parked there—a black jeep with military license plates and a dark-colored limousine. The Mantis got out and pulled the side door of the van open.

"Get out," he said. "It is only a short walk from here."

"Where are you taking us?" Han asked.

The Mantis smiled. "To your reckoning."

THE CABBIE, WHO said his English name was Arnold, had proved adept at following the two vans in the heavy traffic. As they all got closer to the river, the traffic thinned a bit and Bolan watched as the two vans pulled onto a gravel side road. It seemed to lead to a dilapidated series of small ramshackle buildings, the tallest of which was four stories. The structures had virtually no windows and the area looked to be in the process of being razed. Aside from the two vans turning in, it was totally deserted.

"Where is this place?" Bolan asked.

"Old neighborhood," Arnold said. "Pretty soon gone. Boom, and they build more."

Bolan told him to pull just beyond the next curb and stop. He tossed the yuan he'd been holding onto the front seat and got out.

"You want me to wait?" Arnold asked. "You pay more money?"

Bolan nodded, then ran down the embankment toward the rows of dilapidated buildings. A fairly intact sidewalk ran between the houses. Trash, tiles and broken bricks littered the adjacent areas. An old pushcart partially obstructed Bolan's path.

He moved quickly and silently, attaching the sound suppressor to his Beretta. He had a full magazine, fifteen rounds and two more in the pouch on his belt. Plus, he had Grimaldi's SIG with two extra magazines and the small Walther PPS he'd taken from Tai Pang with five rounds left. That gave him seventy-four rounds total. He didn't know how well armed his opponents would be, but he figured he'd be outgunned.

Going in with a low-ammo alert against a larger force, he thought. I have to play it smart, not flashy.

His fingers felt for the Espada knife in his right pants pocket, but it wasn't there. Bolan suddenly remembered giving it to Grimaldi so he could hot-wire the damn truck.

He ducked through a narrow space that had once been a door in the back of the nearest structure. The inside of the place was littered with the detritus of human habitation: discarded clothes, a block of partially crushed charcoal, a few broken plastic toys… Making his way to the window, Bolan flattened against the wall and peered through. Across the street he saw the second van with four tough-looking guys in sunglasses standing around smoking and holding shotguns. Three more vehicles were parked in a shedlike structure with only three walls. The black van that had been used to kidnap Yang and Han sat next to a dark limousine and a black jeep with military license plates. Somebody with PLA connections was here.

Bolan scanned the rest of the buildings but saw no trace of Yang or Han. Obviously, they'd been brought here to meet somebody. Their captors probably wouldn't stray too far from their vehicles. He assessed the chances of taking out the four gangsters from his present location. Doable, but he wanted to make sure it wouldn't alert the others. He backtracked through the house and moved in closer, managing to find another vantage point inside a gutted building almost directly across from the four thugs.

Bolan watched as one of the men took a last drag on his cigarette and tossed the butt into a nearby puddle. One of the others hooked his shotgun under his arm and pulled out a pack, offering a smoke to his companion. As the companion shouldered his shotgun as well, accepting the smoke and then a light, Bolan acquired the initial sight picture. He shot the two who were in the most-ready positions first—head shots—then put two rounds into the congenial smokers. All four of them dropped instantly. To be certain they were out of the picture, he put a round in the head of each one, then stepped through a broken-out window frame on the side wall of the structure. He paused at the corner of the building, looked and listened.

It was a faint sound, but unmistakable: a voice shouting in Mandarin coming from inside the adjacent building.

THE MANTIS WATCHED as General Wong moved in the light provided by the half dozen battery-powered lanterns. The room was almost empty, except for several folding chairs and piles of stacked bricks, which sat in various places like crude furniture. Wong stepped in front of the two prisoners and continued to shout at them. Both Han and the woman were on their knees. It was unnecessary to bind them. Not only was Han's artificial arm now lying discarded in a corner, but they had nowhere to flee. And even if they tried, there were five men here in the room besides Wong and Master Chen.

The general had forgone his uniform in favor of a finely tailored blue suit, similar in design to the one Master Chen wore.

The master and the general, he thought. He would soon be rewarded for serving them both.

"Did you think I would not find you?" Wong yelled. "I have been monitoring your flight the entire time, waiting until this moment."

Wong taking credit for both the surveillance and the capture bothered the Mantis slightly. After all, he had been the one who'd killed Tai Pang, taken his place, perpetrated the masquerade to monitor the Americans' flight and planted the locating device in Han's artificial arm when they jumped from the train. All the vaulted general had done was sit in the comfort of his offices and wait for the notifications.

Wong pulled a Norinco Type 213 from under his jacket and held it to Han's forehead. The traitor closed his eyes, sweat rolling down his face. The girl looked ready to urinate on herself. In spite of the tears and the smudges of dirt, she was rather attractive. The Mantis regretted that she was going to die so soon, before he had the chance to take some pleasure with her.

He smiled. Perhaps he would ask Master Chen for permission to do that. It would be a nice bonus.

Wong cocked back the hammer of the Norinco. "Do

you know the consternation you have caused me? The anxiety?"

Master Chen raised his hand. "One moment, Comrade General." His voice was serene, like the gentle rippling of water over the stones in a brook. "Would it not be prudent to first check the dragon key to make certain it is the correct one?"

Wong's lips curled into a snarl, and he whipped the pistol across Han's face, opening a gash on his right cheek. The blood streamed downward and dribbled onto his shirt. Then Wong poked the pistol into the girl's face. "You will pay as well, for your interference."

Master Chen clapped his hands together once, and then held an open palm toward the Mantis. He reached into his pocket and pulled out the dragon-headed charm that held the flash drive and handed it to the master.

"Ah," Master Chen said. "At last, we have in our possession that which we have sought."

"Give it to me," Wong said.

Master Chen held it toward him and said, "You can verify it on this computer." He clapped again and one of the lackeys stepped forward with an open laptop.

Wong frowned and stuck the pistol in his waistband—without, the Mantis noticed, flipping on the safety. A reckless move for one purported to possess such extensive military training. He pulled at the dragon key, sliding the green head off the metallic plug. The lackey reached for the flash drive but Wong snarled, "I'll do it. Give me that." He snatched the laptop out of the lackey's hands and stepped off to the side. Cradling the device in his arm, he inserted the flash drive, looked around and then punched a series of keys. He waited, but then his lips spread in a smile that showed both triumph and relief. After adjusting the mouse and clicking it a few times, he smiled again. He carefully set the open computer on a clean place on the floor.

"All is well?" Master Chen asked.

"Yes," Wong said. He pulled the pistol out of his belt and strode over to Han. "Now I'm going to enjoy killing you." He pointed the gun at the woman's face. "Or would you rather watch her die first?"

"Please," Han said. "She is—"

Wong backhanded him, using his fist this time. He spat in Han's face, turned and delivered another expectoration into the woman's face.

"I think I will shoot her first," Wong said, "but not fatally...yet. To show you both the pain that comes with retribution and justice."

"You dare speak of justice?" Han said. "When you steal from the poor farmers and sell our country's military secrets?"

Wong punched him again, and then pointed the pistol at Yang.

The Mantis heard a sharp flicking sound, and Wong's head jerked, blood bursting out of his gaping mouth and dappling the two kneeling prisoners, Master Chen and the Mantis. Another whistling, snapping sound and the guard across the room grabbed his chest and curled forward. Wong was twisting, still alive, and brought the pistol upward, pulling the trigger. The end of the barrel exploded with a searing flash, and the Mantis felt the heat of a round whiz by him.

Wong's body jerked again, and this time he twisted to the floor.

The Mantis turned and saw the big American, Cooper, leaning through a broken side door with an elongated pistol, smoke curling from an attached sound suppressor.

Wong's pistol flashed, and this time the Mantis looked in horror as Master Chen suddenly hunched forward, his hands holding his stomach.

"Wong, you idiot," he said.

"Master!" the Mantis yelled, grabbing the wounded man and pulling him down to the floor, out of the line of fire.

Had Wong shot the master accidentally? The Mantis cradled Chen's head. No matter. It was caused by the American, and he would now die.

BOLAN PUSHED THROUGH the broken door, firing as he advanced. There were seven hostiles inside the room, and so far he'd only managed to take out two of them. His old buddy, Tai Pang, was there, too, and Bolan knew how deadly that man could be, with or without a gun.

Swiveling to the right, Bolan shot a Triad gangster leveling a shotgun toward him. The weapon went off, sending a blast of what was apparently double-ought-buck into the dirty floor. Bolan felt the sting of ricocheting pellets sear his left leg. He put a second bullet into the gangster's forehead for good measure, and then jumped to his left to avoid being a stationary target as he scanned the room.

Two more were visible, but where was Tai Pang?

Another thug was firing a pistol. The rounds whizzed by Bolan's side. He brought the Beretta around and shot this new assailant in the throat. As that gangster fell to the floor, Bolan pivoted and shot the one by the door who'd been fumbling with a shotgun. Two more to go—one of them being Tai Pang and the other a guy in a blue suit. They were both on the floor, as were Han and Yang.

The slide locked back on his Beretta. Bolan dropped

it and pulled out the SIG. He began to extend his arm when a foot smashed into his wrist, knocking the SIG Sauer from his hand. It clattered across the dirty floor. Bolan's eyes automatically followed it, which, seconds later, he realized was a tactical error, as a hooking kick caught the back of his head.

Bolan pitched forward, moving with the blow. He regained his footing after a few staggering steps, only to get hit again in the center of his back by a flying kick. This time he went sprawling onto all fours. He pushed himself forward and rolled to his feet, assuming a fighting stance as he turned to face the assailant who stood in front of him.

"Tai Pang," Bolan said, hoping to gain a moment to take a breath. "I thought I'd seen the last of you at the abandoned buildings."

The wiry man spat. "My name is not Tai Pang. It is Lee Son Shin." His body snapped into a kung fu stance, his eyes glaring with hatred. "I am also called the Praying Mantis, and all those who know me fear me. Think of that as you die."

"I'll try to remember," Bolan said. He figured if he could keep his opponent angry, it might offset his game a little.

The Mantis jumped forward, spanning the six feet between them with a seemingly effortless leap. His body twisted in the air, and before Bolan could counter, the other man's instep smashed into Bolan's left shoulder. The blow knocked him off balance, but not down. Bolan figured he outweighed the Mantis by at least fifty pounds, so he had the advantage in power, if he could connect. He shot a quick left jab out toward Lee's head, but the Mantis slipped the punch and spun around, catching Bolan's exposed side with a vicious kick.

Bolan took a step back, and the Mantis pivoted and whirled, smashing another hooking kick into Bolan's back. Pain shot up through his spine. The Executioner tried a quick left hook, but Lee swayed back, allowing Bolan's fist to sail over him.

Two quick, thumping punches collided with Bolan's rib cage, but they hardly affected him at all. The spinning kick that immediately followed did, however. It came out of nowhere and clipped Bolan's jaw. Black spots coalesced in front of his eyes for a split second, then vanished. Taking a quick breath, Bolan lashed out with another left hook, this time catching Lee's cheekbone. The smaller man staggered.

Bolan advanced, popping him with a left jab, right cross.

The punch didn't quite land flush on Lee's jaw, so the damage was minimal. The smaller man rammed a side kick into Bolan's gut, and another sharp pain shot through him. Bolan swung an elbow down onto Lee's thigh. The Mantis whirled and caught the back of Bolan's head with a spinning back kick. The black spots came and went again.

Got to get inside those kicks, Bolan thought.

He saw the flicker of Lee's right eye and the man's foot swept up and clipped Bolan's temple.

The tell, Bolan thought. His eye flickers right before he strikes.

The Mantis stepped forward, sending a snapping front kick at Bolan's face, but the Executioner was ready. He blocked it with his left hand and stepped inside, delivering a powerful right to Lee's midsection. The blow knocked the Mantis backward.

Get inside, Bolan told himself. Work the body. Slow him down.

The Mantis jumped forward again, but Bolan anticipated the move, grabbing the other man's foot and jerking it upward.

This time it was the Mantis who dropped onto the dirty floor, but he recovered with the quickness of a mongoose and whirled. The perfectly executed sweep caught Bolan's forward leg and knocked him off his feet. He hit the ground hard, landing on a pile of partially demolished bricks. Bolan rolled off the bricks just as the Mantis, who was suddenly on his feet again, brought an ax kick down toward Bolan's head.

As he rolled, Bolan picked up a half brick and threw it hard, but his opponent brushed it away with a flick of his hand. It slowed his advance enough for Bolan to start to get up.

The Mantis jumped forward again, his right foot lashing out and ripping into Bolan's left side. As the Executioner tried to pull away from the blow, the Mantis flipped a second kick with the other foot.

Bolan was beginning to feel the ache of being on the receiving end of too many hits. It was time to take the offensive again. He feigned being more severely injured to draw the Mantis closer, and then twisted with a right uppercut as he came in. Bolan's fist caught the Mantis on the chest and bounced off his jaw, sending the smaller man sprawling.

Now it was Bolan's turn to move in. But the Mantis surprised him by flinging a brick that smacked into Bolan's left shoulder, leaving a residual, stinging pain. The Executioner continued moving through it, getting close enough to deliver a solid left hook that connected square on the Mantis's face. Bolan had managed to get his weight behind the punch, and the Mantis went flying. He hit the ground and did a rolling motion, like a reverse somersault, and straightened up on his feet again about ten feet away. His right arm cocked back and then zoomed forward.

Something shiny flashed, and seconds later Bolan felt a burst of pain as a circular throwing star ripped its way up his left arm. He ducked and tossed some more broken bricks at the Mantis, whose hands flashed again.

The *balisong* knife appeared. The Mantis smiled. "I shall enjoy cutting your throat."

Bolan said nothing, watching for the tell. The Mantis jumped forward, slashing at Bolan's left shoulder.

The Executioner dodged the blow and grabbed the other man's right wrist. He stepped closer and used his other hand to grip the knife hand. The Mantis must have realized he'd made a mistake by getting too close. He smashed a palm strike into Bolan's face. The two men danced for a dominant position, but Bolan used his superior strength and weight to pull, then push the knife into his opponent.

It made a popping sound, and the Mantis grunted as the blade pierced his abdomen.

You said you like shiny things, Bolan thought. Here's your last one.

Taking no chances, Bolan forced the smaller man to the ground, continuing to bear down on the knife hand. The Mantis struck Bolan's right temple with a chopping blow, but the punch didn't have much force. Their eyes locked, and the Mantis gritted his teeth, his lips twisting into a scowl, and then his eyes drifted up and to the right, looking vaguely unfocused, and finally sightless.

Bolan stood up, feeling as though he'd been run over by a truck.

No, not a truck, he thought. A Chinese bullet train, maybe.

He staggered across the room and picked up the SIG Sauer and then the Beretta. Shoving the SIG into his belt, he dropped the magazine from the Beretta, inserted a new one and released the slide. He turned and went to check on Yang and Han. He helped Yang to her feet and she embraced him.

"Oh, my God," she said. "I thought I was going to die. They were going to kill us."

Tears streamed down her face. Bolan held her as she cried on his shoulder. He reached out with his other hand to help Han to his feet. The one-armed man's face was a mixture of sweat and blood, with a gash on his right cheekbone and a split lip.

"Looks like you might need some stitches," Bolan said. "How do you feel?"

Han smiled wanly. "I feel grateful to be alive." He bowed. "Thank you for saving us."

Bolan gave a quick nod in return.

"I never doubted, somehow, that you would come," Han said. "And you beat the Praying Mantis at his own game. In physical combat. He was a legend here. Your skill is extraordinary."

Bolan managed a grin.

"How did you find us?" Yang asked, stirring from his embrace. He let her go.

Bolan shrugged. "I tracked you from the bank," he said. "What about you? How are you feeling?"

"I'll feel a lot better when we get out of here."

"I agree," Bolan said. "Let's go."

"Not quite yet," Han said. He stumbled a bit as he scrambled over to the laptop that was lying on the floor and picked it up, cradling it with his good arm. He walked over to a stack of bricks and set the computer on top. His hand poised over the keyboard, he began pressing keys. Bolan could see the screen images popping up. Han smiled and then pressed some more keys. He smiled again and looked at them, grinning now from ear to ear.

"The computer has asked me if I wish to rename the password on the dragon key," he said. "Do you have any suggestions?"

"How about the Shanghai subway?" Bolan said. "Which I hope we can catch to get out of here. I left a cabbie named Arnold waiting up on the road."

Twelve hours later, Shanghai waterfront

BOLAN GLANCED AT the lights of the city, glowing like a myriad of colored jewels, then at the dark waters of the South China Sea slapping against the wharf, and finally at the sleek cabin cruiser that would take them to their rendezvous in international waters with the US Navy. It was the last leg of this journey to get out of China. Despite all he'd been through, Bolan felt as if he was catching his second wind.

The man on the boat jumped down and stood by the moorings. "Are you ready to shove off?"

His accent sounded British, and Bolan figured the guy was probably MI6. He reached in his pocket and felt the hard ridges of the Walther PPS he'd recovered from the Mantis. Bolan would do his best to get it back to Crissey so it could be returned to the dead agent's family. It was the warrior's code. He turned to the others.

"Shall we?"

Grimaldi smiled and took in a deep breath. "Ah, I feel like singing 'A Slow Boat to China' with Frank Sinatra."

"I'd prefer a quick boat out of China," Bolan said.

"Yeah, that'll work, too." Grimaldi glanced at Yang, who was smiling at him. "Did I ever tell you about the time me and him took a skiff out of Singapore with a load of bandits on our six?"

"No, Mr. Grimaldi," she said with what looked like a tolerant smile. "But I'm sure you will."

Both Bolan and Han laughed at that one.

They started toward the stairs that would take them down to the boat. As they reached the pier, Han placed a hand on Bolan's shoulder.

"Cooper-*jun*," he said.

Everyone stopped and looked at him.

"I only came this far to be certain you could leave safely," Han said.

Bolan gave him a questioning look. "What does that mean?"

"It means," Han said, "that I am not yet ready to leave China."

After all they'd been through, the pronouncement surprised Bolan, but he said nothing.

"I will trust you to look to the well-being of my family," Han continued. "And tell them I will join them once my job here is done. I still have much work to do."

"Done?" Grimaldi said. "You're seriously thinking of staying here after a PLA general and a bunch of Triad gangsters tried to punch your ticket?"

Han looked at him and smiled. "I will miss your colorful language, my friend. I think there is much you could teach me about the proper use of English idioms."

"I'll take that as a compliment." Grimaldi grinned and extended his hand. "At least until I figure out what it means."

"But why?" Yang asked. "Why are you staying? They tried to kill you."

Han turned toward her and made a quick bowing gesture. "As I said, there is still much to do here. I have many people who are depending on me to be their voice against the political corruption."

Bolan reached into his pocket and pulled out the thick roll of yuan. "Here, maybe this will help."

Han laughed and shook his head. "Thank you, but it is not necessary." He held up the flash drive. "Now that I have the dragon key decoded and General Wong is dead, I am suddenly a very rich man."

Bolan smiled and shoved the yuan into Han's shirt pocket. "Keep it anyway. You'll need some knocking-around money."

"So what are you gonna do with all that dough?" Grimaldi asked.

"There is a saying in the new China," Han said. "The way to power is lit by money. Few of the rural people here have access to the benefits of our burgeoning economy. I will use this newfound wealth to help them." He shrugged. "Who knows? Perhaps I shall become a politician."

"Nah," Grimaldi said. "You're way too honest."

Han laughed. "We shall see. But let us hope that one day we will all meet again in your Las Vegas. And I would fit in very well, would I not?"

Grimaldi cocked his head, looking perplexed. "Huh?"

Han pointed to his missing left arm. "Am I not, as you say, a one-armed bandit?"

Grimaldi's mouth dropped open but no sound came out.

"You're more like a one-armed swordsman," Bolan said. "The one you told me about. And I owe you a debt of thanks." He turned and pointed at Grimaldi. "This is the first time I've ever seen him speechless."

Han held out his right hand. "Thank you again, for everything."

Bolan shook hands with Han. *"Zhu ni haoyun."*

Han smiled. "Your Mandarin is improving. Good luck to you, as well. I will never forget you."

Han and Grimaldi shook hands again, and Yang gave Han a quick hug. After they'd boarded the boat they looked back at the dock, but Han had vanished into the night.

* * * * *

The Executioner®

Don Pendleton's

PERILOUS CARGO

Ruthless killers race to find a stolen warhead...

The Himalayas become a deadly hunting zone when a nuclear warhead is stolen. Knowing the incident could start World War III, the President sends Mack Bolan and a CIA operative to retrieve the weapon.

Bolan and his ally are up against cunning assassins and several local warlords. These competing parties are determined to reach the weapon first—no matter how many witnesses they eliminate. With the harsh mountain terrain working against them, the Executioner will need to rely on his wits to win this race...because coming in second is not an option.

GOLD EAGLE®

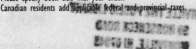

James Axler
Outlanders®

HELL'S MAW

DEATH BLOOMS

Beautiful, seductive and deadly, she is called Ereshkigal. Her flowerlike temple—eerie and alien—rises out of the desolate, sun-drenched desert of postapocalyptic Spain. The river of blood flowing to her temple doors is just the first sign of the horror to follow. With her army of Terror Priests eager to kill for their queen, Kane, Grant and Brigid must confront her dark power. But Ereshkigal's power to control men's lives may prove stronger than anything the Cerberus warriors have ever faced. And this evil interloper will not be satisfied until she has annihilated everything between her and total domination of Earth.

Available May 2015 wherever books and ebooks are sold.

Or order your copy now by sending your name, address, zip or postal code, along with a check or money order (please do not send cash) for $6.99 for each book ordered ($7.99 in Canada), plus 75¢ postage and handling ($1.00 in Canada), payable to Gold Eagle Books, to:

In the U.S.	In Canada
Gold Eagle Books	Gold Eagle Books
3010 Walden Avenue	P.O. Box 636
P.O. Box 9077	Fort Erie, Ontario
Buffalo, NY 14269-9077	L2A 5X3

Please specify book title with your order.
Canadian residents add applicable federal and provincial taxes.

GOLD EAGLE®

GOUT73